MEET ALL THESE FRIENDS IN BUZZ BOOKS:

Thomas the Tank Engine
The Animals of Farthing Wood
Fireman Sam
Looney Tunes
Bugs Bunny
Flintstones
Joshua Jones
Rupert

First published in Great Britain 1993
by Buzz Books
an imprint of Reed International Books Limited
Michelin House, 81 Fulham Road, London SW3 6RB
and Auckland, Melbourne, Singapore and Toronto

Rupert Characters™ & © 1993 Express Newspapers plc.
Licensed by Nelvana Marketing Inc.,
U.K. representatives: Abbey Home Entertainment Licensing
Text © copyright 1993 Methuen Children's Books
Illustrations © copyright 1993 Methuen Children's Books

ISBN 1 85591 2821

Printed in Italy by Olivotto

RUPERT
and the
SILENT FLUTE

Story by Norman Redfern
Illustrations by SPJ Design

It was a wintry Friday afternoon. After school, Rupert, Bill, Algy and Gregory set off for Rupert's house. Mrs Bear had invited them all for tea.

When they reached Nutwood Common,
Algy ran across the grass, then turned
round and threw his tennis ball high into
the air.

"Catch, Rupert!" he shouted.

Rupert darted forward and the tennis ball
dropped neatly into his cupped hands.

"To me, Rupert!" called Gregory.

Rupert threw the ball gently to Gregory.
It was an easy catch, but as Gregory
reached out, he slipped on a patch of mud.
The ball whistled past his ear and fell onto
a gorse bush at the edge of the woods.

Gregory jumped to his feet and skipped
over to the bush where the ball had landed.

"I can get it back if I use a stick," he said,
and he bent down to look under the bush.
"Here's one!"

Rupert, Bill and Algy watched Gregory
use the little stick to free the tennis ball.
Then, to their surprise, Gregory put the
stick to his lips.

"Look!" he cried. "It's got holes in it, like a flute!" And he blew into the hollow stick.

But nothing happened. He tried again, blowing harder this time, but still not a peep came out of the little flute.

"Never mind," said Rupert. "Let's go and see what's for tea!"

11

As they walked, Gregory marched in front, pretending to play his new flute.

"Left, right! Left, right!" he chanted.

Algy decided to play a joke on Gregory.

"Left turn!" he shouted.

Gregory turned smartly to his left and stomped up the path to Nutwood Police Station. All the way he played his wooden flute, but still no sound came from it.

"Halt!" barked a deep voice. "About turn!
Quick march!"

In the doorway of the Police Station stood
Constable Growler. Gregory hurried back
down the path to join his friends. Together
they set off again for Rupert's house.

Mrs Bear was waiting at the cottage.

"I'm sorry we're late," Rupert told his mother as they laid the table for tea. "But Gregory slipped on some mud and — "

He looked round the room. Bill and Algy were sitting at the table, but there was no sign of Gregory.

"Look, Rupert," laughed Mrs Bear, pointing out of the window.

There was Gregory, marching up and down the garden path, still playing his silent flute!

After tea, Rupert waved goodbye to his
friends and went back inside the cottage.
It was a wintry evening, and his father was
putting some more wood on the fire.

"What a funny little log," said Mr Bear,
picking up a stick to throw into the grate.

"Oh, no! That's not a log!" cried Rupert.
"It's Gregory's flute!"

"Here," said Mr Bear, handing Rupert the
flute. "You can take it round to Gregory
tomorrow."

Early the next morning, Rupert heard
someone talking to his father.

"...all the way up the path to the Police
Station!" said a deep, stern voice.

It was Constable Growler! Rupert hoped
that Gregory wasn't in trouble for marching
up and down outside the Police Station.

18

"Constable Growler said that some of his spring flowers have bloomed already!" said Mr Bear after the policeman had gone.

"But it's far too soon!" said Mrs Bear.

Rupert pointed out of the kitchen window. "Look, Daddy!" he cried. "Your flowers are out, too!"

"How peculiar," said Mr Bear, shaking his head. "It's as if they think that spring is here already."

After breakfast, Rupert set off for Gregory's house with the flute. He soon came to Nutwood Police Station, where he found the Wise Old Goat carefully inspecting Constable Growler's flowers.

"Hello," said Rupert. "What brings you to Nutwood?"

"Constable Growler rang this morning," replied his friend. "He's very puzzled about his flowers. And so, I must admit, am I!"

"The flowers in my father's garden are blooming, too," said Rupert. He held out the hollow stick in his hand. "Look at this flute we found yesterday."

Rupert told his friend all about Gregory's
little flute. He showed the Wise Old Goat
how Gregory had marched up and down
outside the Police Station blowing the flute.

His friend chuckled, and then looked
serious.

22

"Oh, dear," said the Wise Old Goat. "May I hear the flute again?"

Rupert blew into the silent flute once more, and the Wise Old Goat listened very carefully.

"You cannot hear a sound," said the
Wise Old Goat. "But to the Imps of Spring,
it is as clear as a bell! This flute is their
special signal to wake the flowers from
their winter sleep. Only they can hear the
music and only the King of the Imps may
play the flute."

"The King must have left it under the bush where Gregory found it," said Rupert. The Wise Old Goat nodded. "And when Gregory tried to play the flute, the Imps followed the sound," he said. "They set Constable Growler's flowers blooming, and your father's, before it was time."

"Look!" cried Rupert. "Here comes Gregory!"

"Hello, Rupert," said Gregory. "I was just on my way to your house to get my flute."

Before Rupert could say anything, the door to the Police Station opened.

"Good morning, all," said Constable Growler. "Now, Gregory Guineapig, I want a word with you! I hear that you like playing the whistle?"

"Oh, dear," said Rupert.

  The village policeman took something out
of his jacket pocket. "Well, try this!" he said,
handing Gregory a shiny tin police whistle.
  Gregory put the whistle in his mouth.
Suddenly, the air was filled with a piercing
sound. Rupert, the Wise Old Goat — even
Constable Growler — covered their ears as
Gregory blew with all his might.

"I must hurry," shouted the Wise Old Goat above the din. "I shall take the flute back to the King of the Imps at once!"

"Please tell him that Gregory didn't mean any harm. He was only playing," said Rupert.

"Even the King of the Imps was young
once," laughed the Wise Old Goat as he
strode off towards Nutwood Common. He
looked back at Gregory. "But maybe not
that young!"

This is for Helen – our own red belt

Scholastic Children's Books,
Commonwealth House, 1-19 New Oxford Street,
London WC1A 1NU, UK
a division of Scholastic Ltd
London ~ New York ~ Toronto ~ Sydney ~ Auckland

First published in New Zealand by Ashton Scholastic, 1995
This edition published in the UK by Scholastic Ltd, 1996

Copyright © David Hill, 1996

ISBN 0 590 13645 3

Printed by Cox and Wyman Ltd, Reading, Berks.

10 9 8 7 6 5 4 3 2 1

Chapter 1

By the time the first round ended, I knew I had it won. I'd been training for this for three months solid; now I was going to win.

His name was Nick. Or maybe Rick; I wasn't sure. I suppose I should have listened harder when the quarter-finals were announced. My instructor, Selwyn, would say so; he's always at us with this 'know your opponent' business.

But even Selwyn could see I was well ahead on points. And even if I didn't know this guy's name, I knew other things about him.

I knew he was slow on his feet. He was shorter and more heavily-built than me; he must have been right at the top limit for a welterweight, like the guy I'd beaten in the second round. I was right at the bottom limit; in fact I could have fought as a lightweight if I wanted to. This guy was a good five kilos heavier than me.

But I was faster than him. My reach was longer, too. I discovered this soon after they called us out — "Welterweight, fifteen years, quarter-finals: Chris Atkinson and Nick . . ." (or Rick or whatever) — and we stepped into the competition area. We bowed to the four corner judges and the referee, and then turned to bow to each other.

In Tae Kwan Do, you always bow to your opponent before a competition bout. You stand to attention with your hands flat against your sides. Then you look your opponent straight in the eyes and you both bow. Some people in our club, like Leon, try staring really hard at the other person so they drop their eyes, but that's just macho crap.

One thing I always do though, is take a quick look at the other person's arms, to see how long their reach is. If you're up against someone with hands reaching down to their shins, then you're in trouble. But this guy had really short arms that hardly came down past his hips. His legs were short, too. He'd have to get in close before he could land any punches or kicks on me. And to do that, he'd have to be fast.

He wasn't. After we'd bowed, we both went into a back stance, weight on the rear leg, holding off for a second to see who would make the first move.

"Go, Chris!" the kids from our club began shouting, "Go, Chris!" I could hear little Brenda squeaking, "Yay, Chris! Yay!" and I could hear Leon getting aggro as usual. "Put him away!" he was yelling.

The other guy's club started shouting, too. "Go, Rick! Come on, Rick!" Yeah, it was Rick. I remember now.

"Fight!" the referee called. Typical referee; stand still for more than a millionth of a second, and he starts yelling at you to get moving.

I tried an orthodox opening, the sort that checks out your opponent's speed without putting you at risk. I went forward with a reverse right-hand punch at his chest, flicking my wrist over at the last moment to give more whip to the blow.

To my surprise, the punch connected. Not very hard, but my knuckles thudded against the leather of his white body-pad, and I knew I'd scored a point straightaway.

You don't expect this in a Tae Kwan Do competition. My opening was such an ordinary one that any green belt would have expected it and stepped back. This guy was a blue belt with a red tab, like me, yet my first punch had landed. He was slow all right.

All this went through my mind in about a second. I'd already ducked back, taken my weight on my left leg, pivoted half round and aimed a reverse kick at his ribs.

That landed as well. Not on his ribs; on his body-pad. We wear so much protective gear when we're fighting that we must look like a couple of sofas on the move. The kick went home with a solid *thwack!* and I knew I'd got another point.

The kids from our club were yelling louder. "Good on ya, Chris! That's the way, Chris!"

So were the other lot. "Keep after him, Rick! Keep going for him!"

He did keep going. I was landing a whole lot of kicks and punches, but this guy kept coming forward all the time. He'd be picking up a few points for that. He didn't even stop when I made contact with him, just moved on through everything. He was solid all right.

But I knew I was getting further and further ahead of him on points. I couldn't do many forward moves because of the way he kept coming at me, but I was able to dodge him easily, and I landed a lot on him while I was moving away. Side kick, hook kick, spinning reverse kick — he was slow enough for me to try them all, and I could tell most of them were scoring points.

Near the end of the round, I even tried an axe kick. This is a move you usually try in Tae Kwan Do only when you're a red belt or higher, but this Rick was so slow I reckoned I had time to do it. And I knew it'd get me a whole lot of points.

For an axe kick, you step back and lift one foot up as high as you can. (Selwyn can get his up almost in a straight line above his head.) Then you bring it down like an axe being swung, so that you hit your opponent on the chest with your heel.

I stepped back, away from the lumbering Rick. I swung my foot up high, balanced myself and brought

6

my foot chopping down, with my heel aiming for the centre of his body-pad.

And *thud!* — he met it with a perfect upward block. Instead of the soft leather on his chest, my heel hit the hard muscle and bone of his forearm. I heard myself gasp.

I felt myself stagger, too. Rick kept his block swinging upwards so that my leg was pushed back and then away to one side. I did a couple of clumsy hops on my other leg and just managed not to fall over. He was still coming forward at the same speed and I was able to dodge away, but I could hear the kids in our club go quiet and the cheering from the other side get louder. Then the gong went for the end of round one.

Selwyn was shaking his head at me when I sat down on the bench. He said something quietly, but I couldn't hear him through my padded headgear and the noise of the others.

"You've got him, Chris!" Wiri and Brenda were squeaking, while Wiri wiped my face with the towel and almost poked me in the eye.

"Why don't you deck him?" Leon wanted to know

Even Janelle, who hardly ever opens her mouth, said, "You're much faster than he is." And Josh, who's nearly a black belt himself, gave me a grin and a nod.

Then Selwyn squatted down in front of me, where I could hear him. He'd been refereeing other bouts early on, so he was wearing his white Tae Kwan Do

7

outfit — his gi — with the black edging round the neck that black belts are allowed to have.

"Chris." Selwyn's voice is quiet, but everyone always pays attention when he speaks, even Wiri and Leon. I ducked my head and gave a little bow of respect, which you do for a black belt or an instructor. "Fight for results, Chris," Selwyn said. "You're showing off. The strong heart wins, not the fast body."

The gong went for the start of the second round. The kids on both sides started yelling again. Wiri and Brenda were loudest as always – bouncing up and down and calling "Go get him, Chris! Go get him!" even when I was still sitting on the bench. Selwyn reckons that one of these days he's going to gag those two with their own white belts.

Rick and I stepped out to face each other again and we went straight into our fighting stances. Once again he started coming straight at me. It was like having a slow, silent grizzly bear chugging after you.

I knew I had to upset his rhythm. I went quickly forward, feinted a punch, stepped back and then came forward again as fast as I could with a roundhouse kick. It landed perfectly, and for the first time he staggered slightly. The cheering from behind got even louder.

I felt the adrenalin rush through me. In spite of what Selwyn said, speed was the way to beat this guy.

I danced in and away from him again. He threw a

8

reverse punch that didn't even reach me, and tried to follow it up with a back kick. But by the time he had his knee lifted, I was back out of range, ready to counter. He stood there looking silly for a minute, then started plodding forward again.

I'd made my mind up what I was going to do. There was one manoeuvre that would get me so many points, I could just stand and look at him for the rest of the bout. I'd have to rely on my speed, and I would. It was all very well for Selwyn to talk about strong hearts, not fast bodies, but I was the one out there, and the fighter is in the best position to know.

I went in and out again, deliberately slower than before. He tried a hook kick that almost got me.

Then, while his foot was still off the ground and swinging, I went flying into a spinning reverse crescent kick. It's a bit like the axe kick – one that only red and black belts usually do. But, hell! I was near enough to being a red belt myself.

I stepped forward and swung my right leg across the front of my body. I spun with the movement of my leg, right round in a circle. Then I jumped at him, my right leg going high up in the air before sweeping down and around to catch him where the padding covered his ribs. It must have looked fantastic.

He blocked me. Perfectly. I don't know if he made a lucky guess or if he read my movements, but his forearm was already up in the air and pushing away. He caught me below the knee and my own momentum almost flipped me on my back. I stumbled, and stumbled again, then tried to get myself back into some sort of defence stance.

Too late. I was so off-balance that he even had time to counterattack. A reverse punch came thudding against my body-padding, with the strength of that solid arm behind it, and I went staggering — staggering into a perfectly placed roundhouse kick. It caught me while my feet were still in a total tangle. I lurched, reeled, almost got my balance back. Then another careful, solid, slow reverse punch landed in the middle of my body-pad, and I sat down flat on my backside.

I'd lost.

In our style of Tae Kwan Do, a bout ends straightaway if one fighter is knocked down. If you go down because you slip, the referee and judges might let you fight on, but this was no slip. I'd been beaten fairly and squarely.

I sat on the floor, and the world felt empty. Three months' training and preparation — for nothing.

My face was hot with embarrassment and shame as I got to my feet. Rick and I bowed to each other. We turned and bowed to the referee and the judges. Then we headed back to our benches, where Rick's club were whistling and cheering and mine were sitting silently.

Well, not quite. There were sympathetic mutters and murmurs. Wiri tried a joke: "He only won because you got dizzy from spinning in circles,

Chris." Leon glared across at Rick's club; Leon hates losing. Selwyn said nothing.

After I'd taken off my helmet and body-pad and the rest of my armour, and once everyone started cheering again for Janelle in the girls' featherweight contest, I mumbled, "Sorry, Selwyn. You were right. I was too busy being a smart arse."

Selwyn nodded. That's typical of him, too; if you've fouled something up, he doesn't pretend it hasn't happened. "You win some, you learn from some," he said. "Anyway," he went on after a pause, "there's always another tournament."

I made up my mind then and there that I was going to win it.

It was a four-hour drive home after the tournament, and the minibus was pretty quiet. Except for Wiri, of course. Brenda and the other kids were asleep. Selwyn was concentrating on his driving. Leon was sulking because he'd lost his semifinal on points. He reckoned he'd won and he complained to Selwyn about it. Selwyn said nothing.

The rest of us older ones were pretty subdued too. Janelle was the only one who'd got a medal, though Josh had come close. Janelle wasn't the skiting sort, but you could tell she was pleased.

I'd already decided what I was going to do after I got home and after I endured noises of sympathy from Mum and Les. I was going to start planning for the next tournament.

Chapter 2

I'd forgotten about the school disco.

I didn't enjoy school discos much in the third and fourth forms and I doubt I'll change my mind in the fifth form. But Mum worries if I don't go to these things, and Les (Les is sort of my stepfather, though they're not married) usually sticks up for Mum, so I kind of got pushed into going.

Apart from being in a foul mood since the tournament, another reason I didn't much want to go was because I didn't have a girlfriend. I was what magazines call 'between girls', which makes you sound like the cheese and tomato in the middle of a filled roll. Okay, not having a girlfriend doesn't bar you from going to a dance, but it does reduce your social status quite a bit.

It doesn't seem to worry girls. They just talk and dance with each other and seem to have a good time by themselves. But guys by themselves stick their hands in their jeans pockets and slope around being cool dudes. Or they thump other guys on the shoulders and make sick jokes. Or they sit on the forms round the sides of the hall with their elbows on their knees and their chins on their hands, being black holes from a distant galaxy.

Just about the first person I saw when I got to the hall was Stacey James. She was with Kevin McAndrew.

That was another disappointment. Stacey came to our school about a year ago. I hadn't ever talked to her much – just a few intensely romantic, heart-stopping things like "Hey, d'you know where we're supposed to go for English?" or "Hey, can I borrow your calculator?"

She seemed a bit snobby, towards guys especially. I saw her coming out of Mrs Jennings' (the school counsellor) office a couple of times. Problems settling into a new school, I suppose. But I thought she'd have had better taste than to be going out with McAndrew.

McAndrew plays for the First XV rugby team and does weight-training. Whenever it's a fine lunchtime at school, he takes off his shirt and sits around so the girls can drool over his physique. One of these days when he does it, I'm going to go up to him and offer him a banana. But not till I've got a clear escape route worked out, and not till I've practised my spinning reverse kick a bit more.

He was being his usual charming social self: 50% macho man; 30% lover boy; 20% pisshead. Nobody's allowed to bring booze to school discos, of course, but there's always guys like McAndrew – or more especially his weaselly mate Dwayne Thatcher – who make a big deal out of getting into their parents' drinks cupboard before they come, or bribing some mate of theirs to go to the bottle store for them.

Big deal! Been there, done that. The last-but-one Tae Kwan Do tournament was held in our town the week I turned fifteen. There was a party afterwards and somebody from another club had brought along some rum and coke. I only had two (or maybe three – or was it four?) glasses, but I know I was starting to talk louder and faster, and I was laughing a lot.

Luckily, it was Les who saw me first when I got home, and he made me go straight off to bed before Mum noticed. At the time, I was pretty slacked off at him for telling me what to do, but next morning I was glad he had.

Guys like McAndrew and Thatcher, though . . . I dunno . . . Thatcher's idea seems to be that you go from being thick to being sick in the shortest time possible.

Meanwhile, back at the disco, McAndrew was

being his usual social self. He was all over Stacey like a randy octopus.

Most kids at school discos don't do any more than hold hands – they're too scared of all the teachers watching. But the moment McAndrew thought there weren't any teachers looking, he had Stacey in a smother tackle.

Even when they were just standing and talking to the others, he kept getting behind her, sticking his arms around her and nuzzling her neck. It made me feel sort of depressed to see it.

She didn't look like she was enjoying it though. Stacey's got long, shiny brown hair that she mostly wears in a ponytail. At the disco, it was piled up on top of her head, leaving the back of her neck all bare and soft-looking. You couldn't really blame McAndrew for wanting to check it out.

She wasn't exactly trying to fight him off – you'd need a black belt to do that – but she was holding herself away from him, keeping her head and neck stiff when he was nuzzling her. A couple of times she caught my eye when I was watching her. (Yes, Chris Atkinson, yes; you were watching her.) But she just looked away again.

I was getting more and more fed up with the whole evening. Hell, I'd only come to show people I wasn't sulking about losing at the tournament, and here I was getting sulkier than ever.

I wandered down the side of the hall and said hi to Josh and a few other fifth, sixth and seventh formers

I knew, and to some kids from the Tae Kwan Do club.

Janelle was dancing with a few of her third-form mates and gave me a grin. She's not as skinny as she used to be; maybe in a couple more years . . .

Leon was leaning against a wall wearing shades and trying to look cool. A third-former in shades at any time is ridiculous; a third-former in shades at a school disco needs professional help. But what can you expect from someone who admires Kevin McAndrew?

I'd had enough. I was going home. I didn't want anyone feeling sorry for me chickening out early, so I started making my way out through the side door of the hall as casually as I could. I was just about there when I heard a noise like a gorilla throwing a tantrum behind me.

It was Kevin McAndrew. "Hey, Stacey!" he was bawling. "Whaddaya doin'? Hey!"

I turned around, and saw Stacey walking fast and straight towards me. Her cheeks were bright and her mouth was tight (and if that sounds like a bad poem, I might add that I got a fright!)

Stacey looked so angry that I decided to get out of her road as fast as I could. The way she was coming straight at me brought back nasty memories of that Rick guy at the tournament.

I scuttled through the door ahead of her. I could still hear McAndrew's voice behind me. "Aw, come on, Stacey! What's the matter? Bloody snob!"

Out in the cool night, with the smell of cut lawns somewhere nearby, I wasn't quite sure what to do. Stacey didn't seem to be in the sort of mood where you could nod politely and say, "My word, aren't the stars jolly bright tonight?" So I kept walking, across the concrete patio outside the assembly hall, down the steps and out towards the front gate.

I could hear Stacey coming up behind me. Even her footsteps sounded angry. I was feeling nervous in case she mistook me for a friend of McAndrew's and gave me a clip across the ear as she went past. I found I was getting ready to shift into a defensive back stance, which was probably taking things a bit too far.

I timed things badly. When our school's front gates are closed at night to keep hoons' cars out, there's only a narrow space between one gatepost and the concrete wall for a person to get through. Stacey and I reached it at the same moment. Being a thoughtful and well-mannered guy, I stepped aside to let her go through first.

Stacey glared at me. Her chin was up high, and even under the yellow outside lights that make people look like walking corpses, I could see that her cheeks were still flushed. "What do you want?"she snapped.

I felt annoyed. It wasn't my fault she'd just found out her boyfriend was sub-human. "I don't want anything!" I snapped back. "I've had enough of the disco and I'm going home. All right?"

Stacey looked away. She shrugged and bit her bottom lip. "I've had enough of it, too," she said. "That Kevin McAndrew—" She stopped and suddenly stamped her foot on the ground, just like a little kid. "Oh, shit!" she exclaimed. "I've left my jacket in the cloakroom!"

"I'll get it for you if you like," I offered. See what I mean about being thoughtful and well-mannered?

Stacey gave an unfunny laugh. "Reckon you could make it into the girls' cloakroom?"

"I could go in disguise," I suggested.

Stacey laughed again, an apologetic laugh this time. "It's all right," she said. "It's not far to my place, anyway." She hesitated, then added, "You live along this way, don't you?"

I followed Stacey through between the concrete wall and the gatepost, caught my jacket on the corner of the wall, tripped on the edge of the footpath so that I almost stumbled into the gutter, and started walking beside her. "Yeah, I do," I casually replied. Meanwhile, a voice inside my head was saying, "Hey, she knows where I live!"

The thump-thump of the disco music faded behind us as we walked on. I didn't try saying anything to Stacey; she looked pretty preoccupied.

"That Kevin McAndrew—" she began again. "What are you supposed to do with someone who behaves like that?"

"You could always try learning self-defence," I said.

18

"You do something like that, don't you? Karate or something?"

"Tae Kwan Do," I corrected her, while the voice in my head chanted, Hey, she knows what I do! Trying to sound intelligent, I added, "It means the hand and foot way."

"You need all the hands and feet you can get with that pig," Stacey muttered. "Can anybody do it? Tae Kwan Do?"

"Yeah, sure, anyone can join," I told her. "We've got kids of eight or nine in our club. And some of them must be — oh, in their thirties, easily." Hell, I thought too late, that'll probably put her off.

We turned a corner. "Are you a black belt?" Stacey asked.

The memory of Rick knocking me on my backside rose up in front of me. "No way," I told her. "If I fight as badly as I did at the last tournament, all I'll ever get is a black bum."

Stacey grinned. "I wouldn't mind giving Kevin McAndrew one of those. Do you learn kicks and things like that?"

"Yeah, but you have to do a fair bit of training first. You've got to build up skills and strength." That'll probably put her off, too, I thought.

Stacey was silent again. I was hoping she'd ask where the practices were, and when, but she didn't.

I could smell her as we walked along. It was a clean, quiet sort of smell: soap and talc, maybe; I'm no expert. We turned another corner. Then Stacey suddenly said, "Is Kevin McAndrew a friend of yours?"

Even though we were in a darkish bit between two street lights, I'm sure my face changed colour. "Hell, no!" I exclaimed. I said it so quickly that we both laughed.

"That makes two of us just now," Stacey said. "Well, my place is this way. Thanks, Chris. See ya."

"See ya, Stacey," I said, witty as an echo. I wandered on along the street while the voice in my head started singing, Hey, she knows my name!

Mum and Les were pretending to watch TV when I came in. "How was the disco?" asked Mum, in that terribly casual, how's-my-little-boy voice she never realises she's got.

"Aw, okay," I replied.

Les grinned at me, and I knew there was a joke coming. "Was it dirty dancing?" he asked. "Or just slightly grubby?"

I stared at him without any expression on my face. Then I saw Mum watching me anxiously, and I felt a bit ashamed. "It was okay," I said again.

Well, the walk home was okay, even if the disco wasn't. And Stacey had thought I was a black belt.

Chapter 3

I didn't get to talk to Stacey at school the next day.
We only have English and PE together because she
takes mainly science subjects whereas I do History
and Geography and stuff like that. Well, I try to do
them. My first term report for History this year said,
"He is rumoured to have contributed in class once."
Let's face it; when they were giving out the brains
they decided to give me good looks instead. Trouble
is, not many girls seem to have recognised that yet.

I did notice, however, that Stacey wasn't hanging
around with Kevin McAndrew. He was hulking his
way about the place with Dwayne Thatcher in tow.
You see a gorilla followed by a weasel and you've
seen McAndrew and Thatcher. But there was no sign
of Stacey; I must have been right about her having
good taste after all.

I didn't think about Stacey much, anyhow. Well, not very much. Tonight would be the first club training night since the tournament, and I was feeling pretty sick about what Selwyn might say. Selwyn never picks on people, but in Tae Kwan Do you have to be perfectly honest. If someone does badly, then the instructor tells them so. I knew I'd fought stupidly at the tournament, and it would serve me right if Selwyn said so in front of the whole club.

At home after school, I sat in the kitchen and chatted to Les for a while. He's looking for a job just now; half-looking, anyway, being Les. He told me about his latest efforts while I ironed my gi.

I hardly think about how strange the gi must look to other people, these days. Back in the third form, not long after I started Tae Kwan Do, I was biking to the club one night and this voice from the footpath called out, "Oooh, who's a poof in his pretty little pj's, then?"

I turned my bike around and faced the voice. It was Dwayne Thatcher, wandering along the footpath with a fag in his hand.

"Sorry," I said, all polite, "were you talking to me?"

He pointed his fag at my gi. "What's with the white pj's?"

"It's a *gi*, actually," I told him, still being polite. "We wear them at Tae Kwan Do. Would you like to come along some time?"

He sneered the Thatcher sneer. "Hell no. Got better things to do, eh?"

I gave him a long, low, level look. "I won't hold you up then," I said, and pushed off. I reckon it was a draw, even though neither of us would admit there'd been a contest.

I forgot about Dwayne Thatcher when I looked at my watch. I put down the iron and quickly put on my gi. I'm not exactly the world's fastest ironer.

Les was chopping carrots in the kitchen and swearing when the pieces went flying. I took another look at my watch, called out goodbye and hurried out to the garage to get my bike.

Fifty metres down the road, my chain broke. I tore back to the house and told Les what had happened. He couldn't resist a smart remark. "Oh, chain reaction, was it?" But he grabbed his car keys and hustled me out to the garage again. He didn't even stop to take off Mum's apron with the pink roses on it. "If the car breaks down, you take the apron," he said.

Les's car backfired and lurched and jerked and got us to the hall only thirty seconds late. "Pick you up at the end of practice!" he called, and drove off in a cloud of blue smoke and an apron with pink roses.

I rushed inside. The others were just lining up in front of Selwyn. Our three 'golden oldies' were there: Frances, who's in her twenties and having a baby in a couple of months; Trish, who's Wiri's mum and talks almost as much as he does; Colin, who's a truck driver and comes whenever he's not driving his rig to the far ends of the country. They don't fight in tournaments, these three; they just come for the training.

I quickly bowed, the way you always should when you enter the training area, then skidded into my place at one end of the front row. Selwyn slanted an eye at me but said nothing.

When lining up at the beginning and end of Tae Kwan Do training, the senior belts go in the front row, the middle belts in the next row, and the juniors and beginners at the back. As a blue belt red tab — three grades away from black belt — I just qualify for the front row.

Josh, a red belt black tab, called us to attention and we all bowed to Selwyn, who bowed back.

"Tournament," said Selwyn, and I felt my face go hot. "Wiri and Brenda — good spirit. Leon — too much anger. Josh — work on the high kicks. Janelle — good speed and good win. Chris — too much, too soon." Again he slanted an eye in my direction.

We bowed again. My face started feeling normal. I wasn't going to be shamed. I don't know why I thought I would be; Selwyn is as hard as a concrete block wall, but he doesn't pressure anyone unless he knows for sure that it'll do them good. I'd already made up my mind that I was going to spend the next three months doing whatever was necessary to win at

24

the next tournament, and Selwyn must have known this.

We started warm-ups. At Tae Kwan Do practice there's no mucking about, no talking unless you're asking something, and you go where the instructor tells you. Tae Kwan Do teaches discipline as well as blocking and kicking.

We swung our arms and we swung our upper bodies. We did star jumps on the spot and we did standing squats for our thigh muscles. I sensed someone wobbling behind me, and heard someone else trying not to laugh.

"Leon – back straight," said Selwyn quietly. "Wiri – mouth straight." The wobbling and the laughing stopped. I didn't look around.

Stretching exercises next: stand on one leg, grab the other ankle and pull it up behind; stand with legs wide apart and push them wider. Janelle and little Brenda are amazing at this – they can do the splits till they're almost touching the floor. The more flexible your arms and legs, the quicker and higher your kicks and punches can be.

"Pattern training," Selwyn announced when we were stretched like rubber bands. "Green belts, in your own time. Yellow and white belts, with Josh and me. Chris, take the new member. Sorry – your name again?"

I recognised the voice from the back row the moment it spoke. "Stacey," it replied.

As the lines broke into groups and gaggles that

25

headed off for various corners of the hall, I swung around. Stacey was standing there fixing her ponytail with a hair-tie. "Hi," she said. I smiled nervously and walked over to her. "Hi," she said a second time. "Hey, love the white pj's!"

I thought of Dwayne Thatcher but somehow it sounded different coming from Stacey. She wore black trackpants and a white T-shirt. The warm-up exercises had left her a little puffed and her T-shirt was rising and falling in a way that made me swallow. "Come for some school disco survival training, have you?" I asked.

Stacey shrugged. "So, what do I do first?"

"First you have to learn the stances — how to stand — before practising anything or beginning to fight."

"Okay," she said, very businesslike.

"Oh, and since I'm your instructor, you're supposed to bow to me before the lesson begins. It's Tae Kwan Do etiquette."

"All right, your Highness." You're not supposed to make cracks like that, either, but since this was her first night I let her off. She put her hands by her sides, bent forward from the hips, and gave me a perfect Tae Kwan Do bow. Selwyn couldn't have done it better. Then she straightened up and poked her tongue out at me. This was a special kind of girl, I decided.

While the other groups around us practised the combinations of blocks and kicks and punches that we call patterns, I showed Stacey how to position her feet and hands for the five basic stances: attention, ready, forward, back, and free fighting.

As usual, I got totally wrapped up in what I was doing; it's one of the reasons I love Tae Kwan Do. Stacey was really quick and cooperative. She picked things up fast and she didn't giggle or talk the way a lot of beginners do before they learn not to. She just concentrated.

When Selwyn suddenly appeared beside us I got quite a shock. I got an even bigger shock when I realised that I was holding Stacey's hand while showing her how to do the open palm block, and that I had my other arm around her waist, making her keep her back straight. She had a nice soft hand, I suddenly noticed. And a nice warm waist. I could feel her ribs heaving from all the effort she'd been putting in. I pulled my hands away and felt silly.

"All right?" Selwyn asked, an amused look in his eyes. He doesn't miss a thing.

"Yeah, fine," I said. "She's getting the idea really quickly."

Selwyn nodded. She's not the only one, his face seemed to say. "Stacey?" he asked.

"Good, thanks," replied Stacey, breathing heavily. Selwyn nodded again and moved away.

"He doesn't say much, does he?" Stacey remarked.

"Doesn't need to," I told her.

In the second part of the evening we went on to counter-training: practising with a partner, taking turns at being attacker and defender. You don't actually land punches or kicks, but you go through all the movements. Selwyn took Stacey away to watch the white belts, since their patterns are simplest. Frances and I partnered off and practised together.

"What's that baby of yours going to say when it's born," I teased, "being bounced around like this?"

Frances grinned. "She's going to be the fittest baby in the country," she said, "kicking her way out of her bassinet at six weeks' old!"

With twenty minutes to go, Selwyn called us together for free-sparring observation. He often does this: he selects a pair, they put on their helmets and padding and try to thump hell out of each other for five minutes or so. The rest of us study what they do right or do wrong.

Selwyn chooses some wicked pairs, though. "Wiri!" he called first. Up bounced Wiri, all eager and excited and trying to keep his mouth shut. His arms were waving about in a dozen directions. "Trish!" called Selwyn, and Wiri's mum stood up.

"Whooo!" the rest of us went.

It was a really good contest. Wiri obviously felt uncertain about fighting his mother, so Trish landed a front kick and a punch on his body-padding before he knew what was happening.

"Go, Mum!" all the girls were yelling. Wiri launched himself into action, legs and arms going like a crazed spider. When Selwyn called a stop,

Trish gave her battling son a huge hug, and everyone cheered.

"Leon!" Selwyn called next. Leon swaggered up. "Janelle!" Selwyn called. Leon looked quite disappointed as Janelle rose to her feet. It was another great choice from Selwyn. Janelle is so quick, and she thinks all the time. Leon just charges in, trying to frighten his opponent.

When he charged in against Janelle, she side-stepped and ducked and dodged so that hardly any of his attacks landed. And when he tried a roundhouse kick that swished through empty air, Janelle flickered forward and rapped a punch against the padding on his chest. It would have earned her good points in a tournament.

"Stop!" called Selwyn straight away. Janelle froze. Leon, red-faced beneath his helmet, started to surge forward again. "I said stop, Leon," Selwyn said quietly.

Leon stopped still. You could have heard half a pin drop. The two bowed and sat down. Leon wouldn't look at anyone. Stacey, who'd ended up sitting next to him, took a quick glance and then looked away. Sensible.

"Chris!" Selwyn called. I stood up. Who was it to be? I wondered. Josh? Colin the truck driver? One of the green belts?

"Me!" Selwyn said, and reached for a set of padding. Everyone burst out cheering. Even Leon grinned.

Sparring with a 4th Dan is an amazing feeling. You know you're outclassed, but you learn so much from being completely thrashed.

I shut everything out of my mind and concentrated only on Selwyn. I watched his hands and his eyes. I didn't even think about my own move; I just let the training and patterns take over, letting my body react automatically.

Selwyn pulled all his kicks and punches so that they landed with only half force. I'd have been sent through the hall wall if he hadn't! And he was deliberately slow in beginning some of his moves so that I had time to counter.

But it was still like fighting a blur. I kept my mind wide open, watched him all the time, flung myself away and sideways with all the speed I could muster, and never dropped my guard. Once, when he purposely halted halfway through a spinning reverse kick, I even landed a side kick on him. He nodded in approval.

When Selwyn called stop, my chest was heaving like a runaway washing machine. Sweat streamed down me. Selwyn didn't seem to be breathing any faster than when he'd started. He nodded again. "Good," he said.

I felt fantastic. I was on a total high. There couldn't have been a better way for Selwyn to give me back my confidence.

We did our warm-down exercises, lined up, tidied up, bowed to Selwyn and said goodnight.

"Great stuff, Chris!" Wiri and Brenda squeaked as they headed for the door. Josh reminded some of us older ones that there was a party at his place on Saturday, and we were all invited.

Stacey appeared beside me as I was putting on my jacket. "That was amazing!" she said. "How long does it take to learn how to fight like that?"

"About twenty-five years, in Selwyn's case," I told her.

"Don't be modest. I didn't mean him. Hey, I really enjoyed tonight," she went on as I held open the hall door for her. Remember my charm and manners? "I'm stuffed, but it was neat."

Les was just pulling up outside in his car. "Would you like a lift home with us?" I offered.

"No, thank you," a voice said from the side. "Stacey's coming home with me." A face like Stacey's, but older and tougher, was sizing me up. The woman's hand held a leash, on the end of which was a rottweiler the size of a small house, also sizing me up.

"This is my mum, Chris." Stacey sounded almost embarrassed. The rottweiler-holder gave me a quarter-nod. The rottweiler didn't. "See ya," Stacey added, and the three of them moved off into the night.

I was left standing on the footpath outside the hall. Les was looking at me curiously from the car. Leon, passing behind me, gave a snigger.

I felt a total dork.

Chapter 4

"I didn't know rottweilers did Tae Kwan Do," Les said as I got in the car. "What grade is he? Red belt with black nose?"

"Ho, ho," I replied. "Hey, did Mum let you come out without your apron?"

Les grinned and started off. I could tell because the backfiring noises and the jerking got worse.

"You didn't tell me you knew Karen James," he said.

"Stacey James," I corrected him.

"That's the daughter's name, is it? No, I meant her mum, the one with the Tae Kwan Rottweiler."

"I don't know her," I told him. "And I don't think she wants to know me."

Les grinned again. He changed gear, and raised his voice above the graunching of the engine. "She doesn't take any nonsense, that one," he said. "But she's not a bad sort when you get to know her. She's on that computer awareness course I'm doing at the Polytech," he added.

"All I did was ask Stacey if she'd like a lift home with us."

"Stacey was born when Karen — her mother — was only seventeen or eighteen," Les said, perhaps by way of explanation. "The father vanished and Karen had a real struggle trying to bring the baby up all by herself. There was another guy later, apparently, but I dunno what happened with him."

"Yeah, well, I was just offering her a lift home," I repeated with as much dignity as I could. "That's all."

Just as we turned into our street, Les's car gave another jerk, then drifted to a groaning stop.

"Hey!" I said, brightening. "Maybe it was the car her mother didn't trust!"

The next morning my arms kept telling me they were sore. All the blocking I'd done against Selwyn had given them a rough time. I was still on a high, though, and decided I'd do some extra weight-training after school that day. I may be fairly quick, but I needed more power against people like that Rick guy at the tournament.

At school, I looked forward to PE. Mrs Jennings (she teaches some PE classes as well as being School Counsellor — a healthy body and a healthy mind, I suppose) had promised us volleyball. That's pretty good practice for Tae Kwan Do because it helps speed up your ducking and turning and jumping. I don't always enjoy PE; McAndrew and Thatcher muck about a fair bit, strutting their stuff to impress the girls. A couple of times they've wanted me to show them Tae Kwan Do moves, and they act a bit heavy when I won't. But Tae Kwan Do isn't something you teach casually to anyone. You either commit yourself or you don't.

There was something else I looked forward to as well: Stacey. I kept remembering how nice her hand and waist felt when I was teaching her the stances the night before, and the impressed look on her face after I'd free-sparred with Selwyn. I also remembered the unimpressed looks on the faces of her mother and the rottweiler.

At school, I'd just walked into the corridor, heading for my first class, when I heard a voice say "Chris?" I know it sounds corny, but a little shiver ran across my shoulders. I turned.

Stacey caught up with me. She was wearing her long brown hair loose. It's really shiny and thick and always looks as if she's just washed and dried it.

"Hi," I said. "Feeling stiff?"

Stacey started to nod, then stopped and massaged her neck. "I've got aches where I never knew I had muscles," she said. "It was neat, though."

"Coming on Thursday?" I asked, and realised my stomach was shivery too. That's the trouble with some girls — they make you feel like you're getting the flu.

"No," she replied, and the shivering stopped. I felt dull instead.

"I'm coming next week, though," Stacey said, hurriedly. "I really want to keep learning it. But I have to go and help Mum on Thursday night. She's got this office-cleaning job; there's just two of them and the other woman's away till next week. I'm definitely coming back though."

"Good." I meant it.

Stacey looked serious and embarrassed. "Chris, I'm sorry about after training last night — with Mum and that."

"No worries," I said.

"Mum wasn't being rude or anything. It's just — well, she's always careful about . . . things." Stacey's voice trailed away and she looked embarrassed again.

I did my stuck needle bit. "No worries." Then I did my stupid big mouth bit. "Les — my step-dad — he was telling me about it."

Stacey's head whipped up. Her eyes had the same expression they had when she left Kevin McAndrew looking silly at the school dance. "Oh, was he now? And what fascinating gossip did he tell you?"

I could have roundhouse-kicked myself. "I didn't mean . . . Les just said—"

"Les can keep his mouth shut!" Stacey cut me off like a guillotine. "He's got no right to go spreading private details like that." She spun around and marched off down the corridor. And even though she'd made me feel a complete idiot, I couldn't help admiring the way her hair bounced on her shoulders as she walked, and how straight she held herself — like a dancer.

To make things worse, I'd just been thinking that I might ask her to Josh's party on Saturday. You know how you suddenly work things out in half a second? I was going to say that Stacey's mum was welcome to ring my mum or Les to check, and that Josh's parents would be there at the party, and so on. Fat chance now.

I didn't enjoy the rest of the day at school very much. First I got a Geography essay back — 7 out of 20. Then our side got thrashed at volleyball — McAndrew and Thatcher were playing for the opposition and kept belting the ball over the net so hard that it just about blasted holes in our players. Stacey was on our side and whenever the ball came to her she hit it anywhere except to me.

I got home after school feeling unimpressed with the world. Mum was at work — she does afternoons in the office at the Medical Centre. Les and the car were out; maybe he was pushing it to a wreckers somewhere. Or maybe he was pushing himself to a job interview somewhere. Mum'd be glad if he was; she reckons Les is too easy-going about life. I just wish he'd lay off the sick jokes.

I ate four slices of bread (carbohydrates are good for you when you're training), and an apple (so is vitamin C). Then I went out to the garage where I keep my weight-training gear.

I'm not into weights for the sake of body building. Doing weights is okay if you keep it under control; you know, just to build up strength and muscle tone and that. But to try and look like Arnold Schwarzenegger? Forget it!

My weight training is circuit stuff; about eight different exercises to strengthen my shoulders, arms and legs. I'm naturally pretty skinny, (though slim is the word I prefer) and the weight training helps me build up more power for punches and blocks. This afternoon I really poured myself into it: shoulder raises, arm curls, step-ups, leg raises. I know it's doing me good when I hear myself gasping. It was doing me even more good this day because it helped take my mind off the mess I'd made of things with Stacey.

Mum came up the drive when I was halfway through, waved to me and said, "Cup of tea in fifteen minutes," and went inside.

I was doing a series of lateral arm raises when Mum stuck her head out the window. "Phone, Chris! Someone about Tae Kwan Do."

I heaved and gasped my way inside and picked up the receiver. "Hello?" I panted.

"Hi, Chris," came Stacey's voice. "Would you be able to pass a message on to Selwyn for me please?"

"Oh—hi—I—um—yeah," I replied, smoothly.

Stacey sounded polite but not very friendly. "Could you tell him I"ll be coming next Tuesday, but I can't make it this Thursday—"

"Yeah, right," I said, still huffing and puffing. "You said you—"

"—and could you tell him I'd like to get one of those white suit things? A ji?"

"A gi," I corrected her. It's my sport, after all.

"A gi," she repeated. There was silence for a moment, except for my puffing. Then, "Have you been running or something?"

"No, just doing some weight training," I told her. I wasn't going to say any more than I had to. My mouth hadn't brought me much success with Stacey.

"Oh. See ya, then."

"See ya." I put the phone down.

"Someone new at the club?" asked Mum as I headed back out to the garage. I could see she was dying to know. Mum worries that either I don't have enough friends, or that I've got so many friends I never get enough school work done, or that I've got the right number of friends but they're all the wrong sort. So, as usual, I told her everything she needed to know.

"Yeah," I said.

I went back out to the garage and did fifteen extra arm curls. Whether it was out of annoyance or excitement, I really wasn't sure.

Chapter 5

Thursday at school was just an ordinary working day. Well, I sort of worked, anyway. Sometimes I think lazy Les's attitude must be rubbing off on me. Still, the teachers are probably relieved they don't get too many of my messes to mark.

We didn't have English or PE, so I didn't see Stacey. Would she have talked to me even if I did? No comment.

I did spot her in the distance talking to Kevin McAndrew once, which didn't thrill me. She only talked to him for a minute though, and in a pretty cool sort of way, which did thrill me a bit. Stacey tends to bite her bottom lip when she's nervous or thinking about something. I noticed it on the way home from the disco. And I noticed she was biting it when she walked off after talking to McAndrew. Listening to him would start any girl thinking — about the future of the human race, most likely.

Thursday night at Tae Kwan Do was a working time, too. Selwyn did what he often does soon after a tournament, and took us all back over our basic patterns. We did them as if it was the very first time and concentrated on getting everything absolutely right. "Make any habits good habits," Selwyn always said.

It was a good, thoughtful session. Even Leon was concentrating. I worked mainly with Josh, who's a bit like Rick from the tournament – slow but strong. And then with Colin the truck driver, who's very slow but very, very strong.

I passed on Stacey's message about coming next Tuesday and wanting a gi. Selwyn nodded. "Has promise, that girl," he said, and slanted an eye at me the way he does. I pretended not to hear.

Friday wasn't particularly exciting, either. Stacey said "Hi" in English (in English class, I mean). I said "Hi" back. End of gripping conversation.

Actually, not quite the end. The class was discussing sexist language and the way in which words often show prejudice against women. I asked a question that Les and Mum had been arguing about one night a while back. "How come at weddings they say 'man and wife'? Why can't it be 'woman and husband'?"

Dwayne Thatcher sneered. (He and McAndrew have been put in different classes as much as possible, and we've got the pleasure of Thatcher's company in English.) "Sick!" he said.

40

"No it's not," retorted Stacey. "Why shouldn't it be that way?" She didn't look at me, but I felt as if I'd scored a point at tournament.

Friday evening I did some more weight training. Les's car was back in our garage — I asked him if the wreckers had refused to take it — but there was still plenty of room for me and my weights. Saturday morning I went for a run and did some very-long-overdue work on school assignments. I found it hard to get really excited about the Russian wheatbelt.

Saturday night was Josh's party. I felt fairly neutral about going but Mum obviously wanted me to. Les even said I could take the car but I told him I wasn't going to put up with threats of violence. I can make pathetic jokes, too.

I have to admit that Mum and Les get on really well together. Les has been with us for four years or so now. He and Mum aren't married, but he's a lot better than my real father ever was.

I didn't think so when Les first came, mind you. I hated Mum spending time with him instead of with me. I hated it when Les tried telling me how to behave. How would you like it if some strange adult told you not to answer your mother back?

I remember once — it must have been when I was in Form One — I went stamping out of the house after some argument with Les, yelling that I wasn't coming back, never ever! I went and sat in the woodshed hoping they'd think I'd run away and that they'd feel ashamed.

After about thirty minutes I got bored and hungry, of course. So I went inside with my nose in the air.

"Hi, Chris. Like one of these chocolate bis—" Mum started to say.

"Hi, Chris. Want to watch some tel—" began Les at exactly the same time. Then they both burst out laughing.

So did I, after a minute. Well, I'd got chocolate biscuits and extra TV out of it, hadn't I?

I don't know where my real father is, and I'm not trying to do the evils when I say I don't much care. He sounds a bit like Stacey's dad, except that mine was married to Mum, and he stuck around for a few years after I was born. He might as well not have, to judge from what Mum says about him and his other women. He sends me a card at Christmas — if he remembers.

I reckon it's a shame that Mum couldn't have any more kids. I know she and Les would like some, although if you ask me they're both a bit past it now — thirty-six or thirty-seven — pretty old for having babies, I reckon. They're like honeymooners half the time, laughing and holding hands when they go for a walk and things like that. I wouldn't mind betting the reason they wanted me to go to Josh's party was just so's they could have an evening by themselves.

Remember how I'd imagined I might invite Stacey to the party, and how I'd tell her mother that Josh's parents would be home to keep an eye on things?

Just as well I'd only imagined it. Josh's parents weren't home after all. I could tell when I was halfway up the drive that it was going to be a pretty noisy night. The stereo was belting away and the house was packed, but things were under control. Josh and a couple of other seventh formers were seeing to that.

I stood around in a corner of the kitchen, talking to a few other guys and making a glass of beer last. I'm in training, after all. I watched the girls and decided none of them looked as good as Stacey. I wondered if she was ever allowed to go to parties, and if she had to take the rottweiler with her.

Then I saw a girl who did look as good as Stacey. It was Stacey. And she was with Kevin McAndrew.

I couldn't believe it! After the way he'd been groping her at the school disco, and after the things she'd said about him on the way home! Yet here she was — looking good, too, in jeans and a big white jumper. She had her hair piled up on top of her head, just like she'd had at the disco.

McAndrew had a beer in one hand and was running his other hand up and down Stacey's back. Stacey was talking to another girl. I saw Dwayne Thatcher trying to give her a glass of something — not beer — but she shook her head, so Thatcher poured it into himself. His face was sweaty and

43

vague-looking, and you could tell this wasn't his first glass.

Suddenly, Stacey stared straight at me across the room. I must have been looking the way I was feeling because her face went tight and she turned away. She said something to McAndrew and pulled away from him. He pressed up against her again and started nuzzling the back of her neck, like he had at the dance.

I didn't want to see any more. I put down my half-finished glass of beer, mumbled something about the loo to the other guys, who were busy talking about football, and eased my way outside.

The night was cool and smelled of cut grass, just as it had when I walked home with Stacey after the disco. But this time I was by myself. Kevin McAndrew! the voice in my head kept saying as I walked down the drive. She still likes Kevin McAndrew!

When I got home, Les and Mum were sitting close together on the sofa, drinking coffee. They looked surprised to see me home so early. "Good party, love?" Mum wanted to know.

I shrugged. "Sort of."

Mum was going to ask more but Les had been watching me and cut in. "Want a hand with some pad-work tomorrow?" he asked.

I'd been expecting some sick joke about party games or something, so felt relieved to have got off lightly. "Yeah. Good idea," I said, and managed a

grin. Then I went to bed, tried to think about training . . . and remembered instead how Stacey had
looked in that big white jumper.

Sunday morning I did an hour's good padwork with
Les. We do it on the back lawn. Les holds a big long
pad like a skinny mattress in front of him, and I try
kicks and punches against it. Sometimes he charges
at me with the pad held in front of him, and I have to
counter as fast as I can. Les is quick for a burly guy
— I reckon he'd be pretty good at Tae Kwan Do
himself if he wasn't such a lazy sod. He says he
believes in being kind to dumb animals and doesn't
want to show me up by joining.

This morning I really laid into the pad. I kept
imagining that it was Kevin McAndrew, and this
seemed to put extra power into my attacks. Les and I
were both out of breath by the time I'd finished.

"You all right, dear?" Mum said when we came
in.

"Yeah, I'm fi—," I began, then realised she was
talking to Les.

While Les had tea and sympathy, I went for a run
to cool down physically and mentally. I've a route
that takes me round a few blocks and past the local
supermarket. Our supermarket stays open on Sunday
mornings now (the more people there are unem-
ployed, the more shops stay open), so sometimes I
get in some sprint training dodging the cars as they
accelerate out of the supermarket carpark.

I was just going past the carpark when I saw a woman struggling with two big shopping bags. She was trying to hold them both while she unlocked the door of a car almost as old as Les's. One of the bags was starting to bend, threatening to drop groceries onto the asphalt.

Always the perfect gentleman, I trotted over, "Can I hold that for you?" I said, and took the toppling bag just before a carton of eggs slid out of it.

"Oh thanks," said the woman. "I thought it was going to be scrambled eggs for lunch for a moment." As she turned towards me I recognised her. Mrs James. Stacey's mother.

She recognised me, too. "Oh, hello. You're from the Tae Kwan Do club, aren't you?" Her voice was quite friendly today.

"Yeah," I said, as a truck engine started up nearby. "Just doing a run so I'm fit enough to survive Selwyn's training."

Mrs James smiled, and her face, which is a tough and watchful sort of face, looked totally different. "Stacey was so stiff the next morning that she could hardly bend down to tie her shoelaces. No, Ham!"

I thought for a second that she'd forgotten something from the supermarket. Then I realised that what I'd thought was a truck engine noise was getting louder, as a big black rottweiler head poked out at me from over Mrs James' back seat.

"Sit, Ham!" Stacey's mum ordered. The truck engine throttled back and the rottweiler settled down.

Two black eyes and a large red tongue still pointed in my direction.

"She picked it up really quickly," I told Mrs James, my eyes on the dog. "Selwyn was impressed."

"Stacey was impressed, too." Mrs James smiled again. "You're the one who was coaching her, aren't you? She said you made everything really clear. Thank you."

Mrs James got into the car and moved off. The rottweiler — Ham — turned his head and watched me out the back window, a thoughtful look on his face.

I ran the rest of the way home with a thoughtful look on my own face. I'd always thought it was pigs that got called ham, not rottweilers.

Chapter 6

By Monday morning, I'd made up my mind about a couple of things.

My priority for the next three months was Tae Kwan Do. I promised myself that after I messed up at the tournament, I owed it to Selwyn, to the club, and to myself to do better next time.

My other priority was to be sensible about Stacey. I realised I was getting more and more keen on her. You never know these things till they happen, but now I had to admit it to myself.

But it looked as if, in spite of what she said, Stacey still wanted to go around with Kevin McAndrew. So I decided to treat her the same as I do anyone else at Tae Kwan Do, and try to ignore how I was feeling about her. Easier said than done.

Especially when all the talk at school on Monday morning was about Josh's party: who'd come with who, and who'd gone home with who, and who wasn't going out with who any longer, and who wouldn't go out with who if you paid them. (Oh yeah? Who's kidding who?)

I hung around the edge of it, waiting to hear what they said about Stacey and McAndrew. I felt like someone who keeps touching a sore tooth to see if it's still hurting. And nobody mentioned them at all! I didn't know whether I was pleased or depressed.

I didn't have to speak to Stacey on Monday. The only class we had together was PE, and Mrs Jennings spent nearly the whole lesson doing a rave about an Outdoor Education Course she reckoned we should all apply to go on during the next school holidays.

Her pep talk was ruined by Kevin McAndrew and Dwayne Thatcher making sick comments all the time. In the end, Mrs Jennings got fed up and chucked Thatcher out, which I thought was a pretty radical approach for a School Counsellor. She told him to report to the Fifth Form Dean. He didn't, of course; he just hung around outside the gym. McAndrew was a lot better without him, as usual.

I had to spend most of Monday night boring myself with the Russian wheatbelt. Trouble was, our Geography textbook had a photo of this neat-looking Russian farm girl with long hair, and you can guess who she reminded me of.

So I went out and did twenty minutes clothesline kicking to try and take my mind off things. Selwyn gave me the clothesline idea. He has a lot of tricky schemes for teaching control and concentration —

punching out the flame of a candle without hitting the candle, or kicking a raw egg someone's holding so that you just hit it without breaking it.

For clothesline kicking, you stand in front of the line and go through all the patterns that have high kicks in them — rear leg standing kick, front leg turning kick, reverse turning kick, axe kick and so on. Each time, you try to get your foot up high enough to flick the clothesline. It really makes you stretch. (If you hit the clothesline too fast and accidentally break it, as I did once, it makes you stretch to think up an excuse, too!)

I took the Russian wheatbelt along to school the next morning, and handed it in to my surprised Geography teacher. As I came out into the corridor I almost collided with Stacey.

We were face to face for a second, and my stupid stomach started shivering again. She looked as if she wasn't quite sure what to say. I gave her a nod and kept going. And I wondered all through the next two classes if I shouldn't have been more friendly.

I got to practice on time that evening, mainly because my bike chain was fixed (thanks, Les), and I didn't have to go in the car (no thanks, Les).

As soon as I got into the hall and bowed, I looked to see if Stacey was there. I looked without looking, if you know what I mean.

She wasn't. There was no one in trackpants and T-shirt.

She was! Over in the far corner, wearing her gi, and looking a bit embarrassed while Wiri's mum Trish showed her how to tie her white belt.

The gi trousers and jacket are floppy and soft, and the belt pulls them in tight around the waist. Dwayne Thatcher was right: they do look like pyjamas. So, yeah, there is a cheap thrill in seeing some of the older girls wearing them. The little ones like Brenda look cute; the older ones definitely look like girls. Stacey looked very definitely like a girl.

I kept my distance from her again, till Selwyn gave the signal for practice to start. He clapped his hands once; everyone stopped talking and got into their rows.

We bowed to Selwyn. We warmed up and we stretched. We all did thirty press-ups because Selwyn was feeling in a vicious mood. Leon did ten more because he'd been sticking his backside up in the air.

"Two notices," said Selwyn when we were all standing up again and breathing hard — all except him. "Stacey — welcome as a white belt." Selwyn clapped his hands once again. We all turned round to Stacey and clapped once as well. She gave a huge pleased smile, and I could see a lot of the others smile back. They liked her.

"Grading," said Selwyn, and we turned back to face him. "Grading in four weeks with Master Kim. Blue belts and up." This meant me. It was a chance for me to get my full red belt.

"Now — pattern training," Selwyn went on. "Chris

and Janelle — white belts. Josh and Leon . . ." I didn't hear the rest of what he said. I should have been concentrating; I'd get 50 press-ups if Selwyn thought I wasn't. But I knew who was in the white belts, and I didn't know if I wanted to take her or not.

Janelle and I divided the white belts into two groups, and she started leading away the group closer to her.

I saw that this would leave me the group with Stacey in it. "You take these ones, Janelle," I said. Janelle came back, looking surprised. Stacey stared straight ahead.

I felt annoyed with myself as soon as I'd spoken. Personal feelings aren't supposed to come into training. I should be able to instruct Stacey the way I do anyone. After all, her Mum had said I'd done it well. Oh well, it'd be a good experience for Stacey to have a third former like Janelle telling her what to do.

It can look weird when you see people learning Tae Kwan Do kicks and punches. They're all lined up facing the instructor, waving their fists and feet at him or her. Meanwhile the instructor is jumping around in front and doing the same movements, calling out, "Swing your shoulders . . . Lift your knee!" like a dancing teacher. As usual, I got completely wrapped up in it. I even managed not to think about Stacey; Selwyn would have been proud of me.

Selwyn took the white belts and yellow belts for

the second part of the evening, and made them puff. The rest of us did sparring in pairs or threes. Josh and Colin and I practised self-defence against weapons. To be exact, we practised what we would do if someone came at us waving a dirty great club. Selwyn is quite clear on this point: "Smile nicely and run quickly," he suggests.

There are other techniques you can try, however, if you can't run fast enough. You get in close, so they can't swing the club or whatever, then you grab the weapon and try to throw the person who's using it.

Tonight, this meant that the attacker kept being flipped in the air and landing on the hard wooden floor on his backside. Since Colin and Josh are both bigger and stronger than me, I spent more time doing this than they did. I suppose it was good breakfall practice — landing and rolling at the same time — but I wouldn't have minded practising it on a waterbed.

One time I missed with my breakfall, landed splat on my back, and lay there trying to remember how to breathe. Colin, who'd slung me over his shoulder with one hand, wandered across and put his foot on me like those photos of big-game hunters with a lion they've shot.

At the end of the evening, I hobbled to my place in the front row. "Hot bath," advised Selwyn.

I tried to bow, and my back, shoulder, left leg and right arm all complained at once. "Aaarrghhh," I said.

Janelle held the hall door open for me as we left. "Help for a poor old man. Hey, Stacey's really good, isn't she?" she said, and skipped off without waiting for an answer.

A truck engine started rumbling just in front of me, and there was Ham the Rottweiler, hanging his tongue out as if he could see dinner coming.

"Hello," said Mrs James to me. "You look as if you've had a busy evening. Hi, Stacey," she said with a big smile, as the hall door opened behind me.

"Hi. Let's get going, Mum," said Stacey. "I don't want to catch cold."

The three of them moved away. I climbed onto my bike after a couple of painful creaks and pedalled home. Last Tuesday, Stacey was friendly and her Mum wasn't. This Tuesday it was the other way round. Can't I do a thing right?

I realised while limping to school the next day that it was all my own silly fault. I'd decided I should treat Stacey the same as everyone else in the club. Stupid. From now on I was going to be polite to her, at least.

I got the chance to be polite sooner than I expected. I wandered towards the classroom block, thinking happy thoughts about the Russian wheatbelt, when I saw Stacey coming across the concrete towards me.

She came right up to me and stared me straight in the eye. It was then I discovered she comes almost up to my chin. The girls' uniform in our school consists of a grey skirt, white blouse and white socks, and when

Stacey stood in front of me, biting on her bottom lip, she looked about eleven. Till you checked a bit closer, that is.

I gave her a weak smile and my mouth started to flap out something. But Stacey went straight over the top of me.

"Excuse me, Chris—"

"Oh hi, Stacey. I—"

"—but would you mind telling me what I've done? Why won't you talk to me? Why do you keep ignoring me?"

"I—ah—I—" I found a few words scrambling round where my brain should be. "I'm sorry. I didn't want to bother you—"

"What do you mean, 'bother me'? Talk sense!"

I got angry. "Look, Stacey, when I told you my step-dad had mentioned you and your Mum, you more or less told me to get stuffed. And anyway — you — Kevin McAndrew — I thought—"

"You couldn't understand why I was at that party with him, right? After what he was like at the disco?"

"Well, yeah. I suppose. I—"

"Well, it's none of your business, but I'd already told Kevin I'd go. He asked me before the disco, and I didn't think it was fair to him to suddenly back out." I must have looked amazed at the thought of anyone worrying about being fair to McAndrew, because Stacey went on, "He's a pain, I know. But he's not all bad. And he doesn't find it easy to get on with girls."

She looked down and bit her lip again. "Anyway," she told the ground. "I'm not going out with him any more. He can practise on somebody else for a change."

My stomach shivered again. I tried some more words. "I wasn't meaning to be rude. I just thought I should maybe back off a bit." We both stared at the same piece of concrete but the concrete had nothing to say.

"Janelle says you're really good at the Tae Kwan Do patterns," I offered.

She grinned an embarrassed sort of grin. "I need to do a lot of kicking practice. Janelle can get really high."

And suddenly I heard my mouth setting off on a trip of its own. "Look — if you want to, I've got a training thing at home to help with kicking practice. If you want to come around and try . . . if it's okay with your Mum —" Oh, hell! "— I'd be glad to help."

There was a pause. My stomach knotted.

"I'll give you a ring after school, can I?" Stacey said.

"Yeah, fine. Great. Yeah, sure." Why are you saying the same thing three times? the voice in my head wanted to know.

In Geography that morning, I found I'd got 17 out of 50 for my assignment on the Russian wheatbelt, along with a comment from the teacher: "So that's what your handwriting looks like." Yeah, fine! Great! Sure! I kept saying to myself as I looked at it.

Chapter 7

"Someone from the club might be ringing up about coming round for some practice," I told Mum when she got home from work that afternoon. I didn't tell her I'd already been sitting there for the last half hour waiting for the phone to ring.

Mum nodded. I helped her unpack the groceries and put them away while we agreed it would be a good idea if Russia stopped growing so much wheat. I was on my way out to the garage to prove to myself that I'm not the sort of guy who just sits around waiting for the phone to ring, when Mum said, oh-so-casually, "The same someone from the club who rang last week with a message for Selwyn?"

Aw, Mum, leave it alone, I said silently. "Yeah, could be," I said aloud, and kept going.

I'd done about ten bench-presses with the weights when Mum called out from the house. "Someone from the club is on the phone, Chris. Someone about coming round for some practice."

I did another bench-press to show I was in no hurry. Then I dropped the weights and sprinted inside. "Hello?" I said to the telephone.

"Hi, Chris. It's Stacey."

My stomach already knew it was. "Hi, Stacey."

"Sorry, I can't come around and practise kicking you. Kicking with you, I mean!" She giggled, and I realised she was nervous. My stomach, which had stopped shivering and started sinking, did a U-turn and started coming up again. "It's my turn to cook dinner this week while Mum's at work," Stacey went on. "But can I maybe come round at the weekend sometime? I'd really appreciate the help."

"Yeah, sure. Great. Yeah, fine." I seemed to have heard those words before. I hung up, said "Ta, Mum," and went back out to the garage before she could ask any more Mum-type questions.

"What's this grading that Selwyn was talking about?" Stacey wanted to know at school on Thursday.

"Oh, it's like an exam to see if you're ready to move up to the next belt or the next tabs," I said. "Master Kim comes to the club every couple of months and tests a few people. You have to go through all your patterns, and he gets you to do different moves. And you usually have to spar against some of the others."

"Do you have to break boards? Like on TV?"

"Nah," I told her, "that's not really important. It's the moves and the sparring that really matter. That's what I have to practise from now on."

"Got a long way to go, haven't I?" Stacey said.

"It's taken me nearly four years to be ready for red belt grading," I said. "Be another year before I'm ready to try for black tabs. But every step up feels neat."

"Yeah, I can imagine. See ya tonight then, Chris."

Stacey turned left to go to Chemistry or something, and I turned right to go to History. I looked back after her, and saw Kevin McAndrew standing there, watching me. Tum-te-tum . . .

Training that night was excellent. We did lots of pad work and speed work. The hall was full of feet and fists smacking against the pads, and voices yelling "Tae Kwan!" as they hit. You're supposed to do that; it helps release your energy in one burst. I sneaked a few looks at Stacey and could see how hard she was concentrating. Her bottom lip was nearly getting chewed off.

We had some more free-sparring observation to finish the evening. Everyone waited to see what pairings Selwyn would come up with this time.

First he called Trish. Then Frances, who patted her growing stomach and said "Should I?"

"Right," agreed Selwyn. "One-and-a-half against one isn't fair. Janelle instead." It was a neat contest to watch: Janelle's speed against Trish's cunning.

"Josh!" Selwyn called next. "And Leon." Another excellent pairing. Josh the red belt black tab is much better than Leon, who's green belt blue tab, but Leon has lots of determination in spite of all his macho talk. He stood up well against Josh, and there were cheers when they both sat down. You could see Leon felt great after looking silly against Janelle last week.

"Chris!" called Selwyn. I stood up and bowed to him. Who's gonna bruise me tonight? I wondered. "Wiri!" A figure in a white belt jumped up, waving about ten arms and legs.

I enjoyed the next few minutes. Wiri's got all the energy and willingness in the world; he just needs to think things through a bit more. Three times he rushed in too fast and left a gap. Three times I was able to land a front kick on his body-pad. Then I said "Plan!" (You're allowed to talk to white and yellow belts when you're sparring with them.) The fourth time he came in he was more careful. I went for another front kick, he had his arms ready to block, and he pushed me away well. "Good!" I said, and he grinned so much his face nearly turned inside out.

At the end of training, Selwyn wanted to talk to those of us who were going to do grading, so I stayed back.

"You were neat with that little kid," Stacey told me as she went out the door.

"Why the big smile?" Selwyn asked me a couple of seconds later. As if he didn't know!

Have you ever noticed how, whenever you've got something to feel pleased about, something else comes along and spoils it?

Friday at school was like that. I turned up in a really good mood. Even being set an assignment in History on 'The Origins of the Education System' didn't ruin it — not completely. Then came PE.

The trouble with Mrs Jennings in PE is that she's too buddy-buddy with everybody. Okay, teachers should be friendly. And okay, Mrs Jennings is the school counsellor too. But she tries too hard to be on the kids' level all the time. She's always bouncing around making jokes and the kids don't always respect her.

This day, she wanted us to play volleyball again. I was quite keen, but as usual McAndrew and Thatcher were being a pain. They wanted to do some of the self-defence stuff from a video Mrs Jennings showed us a few weeks back. I reckon McAndrew just wanted to show off his muscles.

Mrs Jennings tried to tell them that they'd need a proper instructor, but Thatcher kept stirring. "We've got Black Belt Atkinson or whatever here," he said, pointing in my direction.

Mrs Jennings looked hopefully at me but I shook my head. We've been through all this before. You don't teach Tae Kwan Do unless it's done properly, with people serious about learning the whole thing.

"Atkinson's no use!" McAndrew butted in. "Anyway, we don't need him. Stacey can tell us all about it, can't ya, Stacey?"

Stacey shook her head, too. "I don't know anything yet."

"Aw yeah?" Thatcher sneered. "That's not what you reckon, eh Kev?"

I stood up and everyone looked at me. "Let's play volleyball," I said.

"Yes, come on everyone!" Mrs Jennings agreed quickly. "Self-defence some other time."

"Shit!" said Kevin McAndrew, and you could tell he didn't care whether the teacher heard him or not. But he got up and moved away with the rest. I couldn't give a stuff what he thought. I knew Selwyn would have approved of what I did.

Stacey asked if she could come around about eleven o'clock on Saturday morning. "Mum says she's doing a Polytech computer course with your step-dad," she said, and I remembered Les telling me the same. "She was quite pleased when she found out who he was."

"Is she after a job with computers then?" I asked.

"No, she's a geriatric nurse," Stacey said. "She looks after old people. But she's been out of work since the hospital had to cut its staff. Money's getting a bit tight, so she had to sell our car the day before yesterday. Now she's looking for any new skills and jobs she can."

Just like Les, I thought. Well, sort of like Les, anyway.

I got up really early on Saturday — early for me, anyway — about quarter to ten. Mum and I aren't always on the best of terms in the mornings. She reckons if I stayed in bed any longer at the weekends, my arms and legs would wither away and fall off. So she was a bit startled this Saturday.

I washed my hair and had a specially careful shower till Mum banged on the door and yelled to leave some hot water. I'd do the same for any visitor, honestly.

Then I tried talking to Les about 'The Origins of the Education System'.

"All I know is that it didn't teach me how to keep a job," Les said. He was being serious for once.

I had made up my mind that I wouldn't start worrying about whether or not Stacey was coming till quarter past eleven. But at five minutes to, I was already worrying. At one minute to eleven, the doorbell rang.

"Someone from the club coming round for some practice?" asked Mum, all innocence, as I stood up.

Stacey was wearing trackpants and a T-shirt that read 'SAVE THE WHALES — I want one for pudding'. "Do I bow now or when we start the lesson?" she asked.

Mum and Les were really friendly towards Stacey. Mum seemed relaxed straight away. Les, of course, had to make a couple of pathetic jokes about how he couldn't kick his way out of a paper bag, and how he used to think Tae Kwan Do was a Chinese takeaway. Stacey seemed a bit unsure of him; maybe she felt he had no right to tell me about her and her mum that time, which he didn't really. But she was polite.

"Come in if you'd like a Coke or something when Chris has finished bullying you," Mum said to her after a while.

"Thanks, Mrs Atkinson," Stacey replied. I liked hearing her say that.

I took Stacey out to the back lawn to introduce her to the clothesline. "Welcome to the country's leading outdoor Tae Kwan Do training centre," I told her. I'd thought that up in the shower.

Stacey looked at the line. "Hey, we've got a training centre just like this at home," she said. "Except ours has got my school socks hanging on it. Sex-ee!"

She pulled her hair up to tie it into a ponytail. Her arms were up over her head and that lifted her — her front. Suddenly I couldn't remember what moves we were going to practise.

To start with, I got her to do some warm-up exercises and stretches. Stacey can do the splits almost as well as Janelle and Brenda; she's really supple.

Then we started on the kicks. I didn't expect her to get anywhere near the clothesline, so I'd hung a body-pad from it at about the height of a person's chest, and Stacey aimed for that.

The secret of Tae Kwan Do kicking is balance. Whether you're standing on one leg or jumping in the air, you have to be balanced so that all your energy goes into the kick — and so that you don't land flat on your back.

At first I had to hold her till she learned how to balance herself.

"This is the sort of thing they warn us about when we have a girls' assembly, you know?" she said, a bit uncertainly. I was crouched with one arm around her middle and the other hand quite a long way up on the back of her leg.

I didn't know what to say. I'd been concentrating on the Tae Kwan Do and hadn't given much thought to where my hands were. "Remember, you've got to start with the hips," I gabbled, blushing.

Stacey started to laugh. "I'll tell Mum that!" she said. Then she must have noticed the colour of my face and looked embarrassed. "You really are a good instructor, Chris."

Stacey was excellent; a natural. I felt quite jealous — she already had a balance and timing that took me about two years to learn. After just two weeks — and twenty minutes today — she was doing rear leg turning kicks, where you spin away from your opponent and then lash back at him. And she was almost reaching the top of the hanging pad. I reckon she learned as much in this one session as most people learn in a month. I could tell she'd soon be streets ahead of the other white belts.

I think we'd have kept going if Mum hadn't called out from the house, "That's enough now, Chris. Poor Stacey'll be exhausted. Come and have a drink. He'll keep you going till it's dark otherwise, Stacey!"

"You can certainly reach with those kicks," I told

Stacey as we did a couple of minutes of warm-down exercises. "You should try high jumping."

Stacey pulled a face. "I tried to high jump a barbed wire fence when I was nine," she said, "and I've still got the scar on my bum!"

Inside, over a Coke, Mum did most of the talking. I just sat and listened mostly. So did Les; Mum must have said something to him while we were outside. And I watched Stacey.

Stacey and Mum talked about food they like — pizza and vegetarian things for Stacey — and Stacey's Mum's job. Mrs James goes to the library three times a week and looks at the regional newspapers for nursing jobs anywhere in the country. I didn't like the sound of that, I have to admit. Les said Mrs James was a dab hand with computers.

It was all friendly and relaxed, with the sun flooding into the kitchen, and I was really enjoying it. We must have been sitting there for half an hour when Les suddenly glanced at his watch and said, "Chris! Look at the time!" Everyone stared blankly at him. "You're supposed to be picking up your new mouthguard, remember? And the chemist closes at two o'clock on a Saturday."

"Oh hell, yeah, that's right." I stood up quickly.

Stacey stood as well. "I'd better go, too," she said. "I've got about a million assignments to finish this weekend. Thanks very much for the Coke, Mrs Atkinson. And thanks for the training, Chris; it was great. See ya Monday." And she was gone.

"Nice friendly girl," said Les. "Pretty eyes."

"She's quite a sweetie," said Mum. "Lovely hair."

They both looked at me expectantly. I knew they would, and I had my answer ready.

"What do you expect?" I said. "She does Tae Kwan Do." I felt bouncy and happy. Nothing could beat me.

Les looked at his watch again. "I've got to go into town myself," he said, "so I'll give you a lift in the car. You can catch the bus back."

A lift in the suicide saloon? See what I mean about how when you're feeling good, something always comes along to spoil it?

Chapter 8

Les's rustmobile got me to the chemist's in time — just. It stalled at a couple of intersections, and took about six goes to get it started again, while I slid down in the passenger's seat and pretended I wasn't there. Les parked just along from the shop and as I got out I saw a meter attendant walking towards us, holding her notebook and looking hopeful. Even if it's only been standing still for ten seconds, Les's car always manages to look as if it hasn't moved for ten months.

The new mouthguard was to replace the one I dropped and broke on the hall floor at training. It's not compulsory to wear a mouthguard for sparring and competitions, but you're an idiot if you don't. Kicks and punches can accidentally land on people's faces and if your broken teeth and fillings start falling on the floor they can give your bare feet a nasty scratch.

On the bus coming home from town, I tried to work out how I could tell Stacey I was keen on her. I'm not exactly shy — not like some people who won't even ring up the automatic weather forecast in case a live person answers — but telling someone that you like them is not an easy thing to do.

The way it usually gets done at our school is that you drop heavy hints to a friend who knows a girlfriend of the girl you like. Then you hope the hints get passed on, hope the girl likes you, and hope she'll send back some hints of her own.

The only school contact Stacey and I have in common is Kevin McAndrew, so I couldn't really see the pass-it-on method being terribly successful. And I certainly didn't think I could rely on Les to put my case with Stacey's Mum. I decided to work on Plan B instead. The problem was that B stood for Blank.

I thought about it on and off throughout the weekend, in between running and weight training and clothesline kicking and the origins of the stupid education system. I did my weight training outside because Les was giving his car a heart transplant, and the garage kept filling up with blue smoke.

There were only three weeks till grading; two and a half months till the next tournament; four weeks till the school holidays. It was too early to start psyching myself up for the first two — the important two — but I kept telling myself that I wasn't going to fall flat like I did with that Rick guy last time.

69

I hardly saw Stacey at school on Monday. We met in the corridor once. She was with some other girls; I was with some other guys. She gave me a smile that went straight to my stomach. A bit further along the same corridor I met McAndrew. He was with Thatcher and he didn't give me a smile.

I hardly saw Stacey at school on Tuesday either. But it didn't matter, because the one time I did see her was first thing in the morning, before History. She gave me another smile and said, "See you at practice tonight, blue belt." I don't think I heard a single thing anyone said in History.

"Six practices till grading for blue belts and up," Selwyn said that night after warm-ups and stretches. "Individual assessment tonight."

Individual assessment means that Selwyn spends about ten minutes with each person who's going for grading. In that ten minutes Selwyn says about three sentences. In those three sentences he tells you about twenty things.

Meanwhile, the green belts and below were practising their patterns under Trish and Leon, with a bit of help from Frances, whose stomach seems bigger at every practice. Selwyn made a point of going across to Leon after a bit and saying, "Good. Well explained."

Leon tried not to look pleased, and he took his group even more carefully after that. He'd be a reasonable sort of kid if he didn't try to behave like McAndrew too much of the time. Stacey was in his group and again I noticed how hard she was working. She already looked nearly as good as some of the yellow belts.

By the time the last half hour came, Selwyn decided he'd earned some training of his own. He runs or practises by himself every night, of course, but he doesn't often train and spar with us at the club. He's usually too busy instructing.

Selwyn's idea of a nice, easy half-hour's training is to spar against everyone in turn — in pairs or threes.

He started the hard way; against Josh, Colin the truck driver and me. It was the hard way for us, I mean. Josh managed to connect with a couple of spinning back kicks, and I think I landed one decent punch. I couldn't be sure because Selwyn was moving so fast. At the end of five minutes Colin was hopping on one leg as Selwyn had hit his knee with a low roundhouse kick; my right hand was aching where Selwyn blocked it as I'd tried for another punch; Josh was just getting up off the floor for the second or third time. I think Selwyn might have been breathing a tiny bit harder than when we started.

We three bowed, limped away and sat down. Three others stood up and prepared to meet the same fate. And so it went on. Selwyn made sure Leon did plenty of attacking and defending when it was his turn, so that he felt important.

Finally, Selwyn took on five white and yellow

belts at once. Actually, it'd be more like six if you counted the extra arms and legs Wiri seems to have when he's sparring.

The lower grades are in fact the hardest for Selwyn to spar against. He has to be careful not to hit them hard, and has to watch their attacks in case they hurt themselves against his blocking. You can learn heaps from watching him.

However, I wasn't watching him as much as I was watching Stacey. For a new white belt she really is something. She was punching and kicking with the rest of them — she didn't manage to hit Selwyn at all, but she didn't miss by any more than the others did. Her teeth nibbled away at her bottom lip (she'll need a mouthguard for competitions) and her ponytail swung crazily around her head. When she kicked, I couldn't help noticing all the curves in her legs and body. Hell! I started concentrating on Selwyn instead.

As soon as I looked away there was a smack and a gasp and I looked back to see Stacey on her side on the floor. Wiri had missed Selwyn with his ten-millionth kick, hit Stacey instead, and knocked her sideways. She landed with one foot twisted beneath her.

It really hurt, I could tell. I wanted to rush over to see if she was okay but Selwyn was miles ahead of me. He stopped the others with one word and strode over to Stacey. He helped her sit up and felt all over her foot. "No breaks," he said, and grinned at her.

Watch it, Selwyn!

Selwyn and Trish helped Stacey to one of the benches at the side of the hall. Trish went off to get an ice pack while Selwyn directed the rest of us through our warm-down.

"How are you getting home?" I heard him ask Stacey as everyone headed for the door. I came over to check on the casualty, followed by Frances and a rather upset Wiri.

"We haven't got a car," Stacey said. She still looked a bit shaky. "Mum and Ham—"

"Les and I can give you a lift." I was impressed by my own quick thinking. "Only take me two minutes to bike home and get him." Selwyn nodded.

As I stepped outside the hall a truck engine started up. "Oh, Mrs James," I said to the figure on the other end of the leash. "Stacey's twisted her foot. I was just going to get my step-dad to give her a lift home." The truck revved steadily.

Mrs James hesitated. "I — oh, you mean Les — yes, that'll be fine. Thank you. I'll see how she is. Stay, Ham!" She vanished into the hall. The truck throbbed on.

"Stay, Ham!" I echoed, and jumped on my bike. The two-minute ride home took me forty-five seconds. I was terrified someone else would give Stacey a lift in the meantime.

Les managed to control himself pretty well. "Some girls are always putting their foot in it," he groaned. "Come on, I'll get the keys."

73

I grabbed a jersey from my room and came back out to the living room where Les and Mum were grinning at each other.

The heart transplant must have worked, because Les's car reached the hall without stalling once. Stacey, her mum and the rottweiler truck were waiting outside.

"I told Selwyn to lock up. Said you were giving me a lift," Stacey said. "Thanks, Chris."

I nearly patted Ham but he looked at me and I chickened out.

Les and Mrs James greeted each other like old friends.

"Hello, Karen."

"Hi, Les."

As Les put out his hand to help Stacey into the back seat, Stacey seemed to stiffen. Her foot must have given her a bit of a stab. "It's all right, Stacey," said Mrs James quickly, taking her by the elbow.

Les and I got in the front and Ham joined the Jameses in the back. Of the two engines in the car, Ham sounded the more powerful. I sat very still.

Stacey lives only about a kilometre away from us but I hadn't been past her place before. Mrs James told Les where to go and it turned out to be the end flat of a block of three. Heavy metal music blasted out from the front flat. Mrs James went ahead with Ham to unlock the door.

"You give Stacey a hand, Chris," Les said. "I'll get her jacket and things."

Stacey got out of the car then cautiously held my hand while she stood. I put one arm around her waist and supported her while she half hopped, half limped up the path. Her hip was near mine; I could feel the movement and warmth of her. Her hair in its ponytail kept swinging towards me as she hopped and I could smell apple shampoo. I wished the path to her front door was twenty times longer.

Mrs James took over at the door. "Thanks very much, Les — and Chris," she said. "Looks like a few days off Tae Kwan Do for this one. Maybe a few days off school, too."

"Janelle!" Stacey exclaimed suddenly. "Janelle was going to lend me a book about basic patterns and that."

"I'll tell her," I said.

"Thanks, Chris." Stacey was standing against the doorway on one leg. "Thanks, Mr—er—"

"Les," said Les. "Take care of that foot, Stacey. Chris needs the instructing practice. 'Night, Karen."

We all said goodnight and Les and I headed back to the car. The rustmobile suffered another coronary about a hundred metres from our place. I finished Tuesday's Tae Kwan Do practice by pushing it the rest of the way back to the garage.

Chapter 9

I lay awake that night, thinking. Not about grading or the next tournament, like you might expect. Not about History or Geography or English either. About Stacey.

Tae Kwan Do is supposed to help you focus your mind, but I couldn't concentrate on a single thing about Stacey. My mind kept wandering around in circles and detours and spirals.

I wanted to kiss her. I even pictured myself doing it, though my picture was pretty hazy about the where and when . . . and about the how. I'd only ever kissed one girl before, and that wasn't very successful.

I kept remembering how her body moved when she put her hair up and when she was practising. I could remember exactly what her waist and hip felt like when I helped her up the path to the flat. Okay, she's not the best-looking girl around. Mum and Les were right about her having nice hair and eyes, but there are other girls in the fifth form who'd have more chance in a beauty contest. Still, she looked great to me.

It wasn't just physical, though. I mean, okay, I'd probably like to do more than just kiss her (Come on, Chris Atkinson, be honest! You know you'd like to do more than just kiss her!), but I like just talking to her, even if we haven't said all that much yet. I like instructing her at Tae Kwan Do. I like being with her. It was cool, that Saturday morning when she came around to our place, and I hoped that sort of thing would happen again.

Stacey wasn't at school on Wednesday. The other Tae Kwan Do kids must have been talking about it, because Kevin McAndrew stopped me in the corridor after Geography. (Industry of the Urals this time. I know now that the Urals aren't a men's toilet.)

"Hey, Atkinson," he said. "I hear you've started knocking girls around at your Tae Kwan Do club now."

"Only in the mating season," I replied. To my surprise he grinned. I grinned back.

"Fair enough," he said.

Then another voice sneered from beside me. "Atkinson wouldn't know what a mating season is. He thinks babies come from under toadstools, don't you Atkinson?"

"Under a fungus in your case, Thatcher," I said.

McAndrew grinned again, then sloped off after Thatcher. Sometimes McAndrew is almost reasonable by himself, but the two of them together are bad news.

I gave myself a really hard training session at home that night. Only five club practices till grading. I did weights and clothesline-kicking. I did ten minutes solid foot-springs, jumping backwards and forwards and sideways on one foot after the other, pushing as hard as I could each time. It's great practice for launching into kicks, but you end up absolutely stuffed. I was heaving and sweating and my ears were buzzing. It felt good though; I was still getting a spring in my legs, even at the end.

No Stacey at school on Thursday either. No comments from McAndrew and Thatcher. I suppose one partly made up for the other. I wondered if maybe I'd give Stacey a ring after school. I had a reason, after all; I was going to ask if she wanted me to pass on any message to Selwyn. Anyway, why shouldn't I just ring up and ask how her foot was?

Janelle made the decision for me. She came up to me during lunchtime, with a bunch of her mates. Funny how third formers always travel in packs.

"Hey, Chris! I'm supposed to give this Tae Kwan Do book to Stacey. D'you know when she'll be coming back?"

"Nope . . ." Suddenly my brain got into gear. "I'll take it if you like. No problem for me to get it to her."

"Oh, okay, that'd be good," said Janelle, and passed it over. As she and her mates moved off she grinned at me over her shoulder. "Didn't think it'd be a problem," she added. Cheeky brat.

The moment we finished our last lesson for the day I set off for Stacey's with the book. Like I told Janelle, it was no problem. Just half an hour's walk there and back. No, I didn't have my bike. Fifth formers don't ride bikes to school; it's not cool.

In the daylight I could see that the Jameses lived in one of the poorer parts of town. Our place isn't all that flash but the streets around Stacey's were full of houses with kids' toys scattered across scruffy lawns; big dogs lying on footpaths; old cars parked up on blocks out front; squares of hardboard patching a few broken windows — that sort of thing. It didn't bother me; Mum always says it's not what people live inside that matters, it's what lives inside them. Good one, Mum.

As I got closer I started to feel nervous about arriving at Stacey's without even ringing first. She might think I was being pushy. Mrs James and Ham might think I was being pushy. But I wasn't going to back out now.

Voices in the end flat of the block were having an enthusiastic 'discussion'. Words I hadn't even heard from Thatcher and McAndrew were turning the air blue, then purple. I walked past quickly and knocked on Stacey's door.

Boom! Boom! roared something behind the glass.

I hoped I wasn't about to become a Ham sandwich.

I waited. Nothing else happened and I felt a bit disappointed. Maybe I should just leave the book in the letterbox, I thought. Then the door opened, and there stood Stacey. She wore jeans and a black T-shirt, and she had a bandage on one foot. Her hair was in bunches on either side of her head.

"Hi," I said. I'd practised my opening speech on the way round. "Janelle asked if I could drop this Tae Kwan Do book off. She thought you might be wanting to look at it."

"Oh, hi!" said Stacey. "Thanks, Chris. Hey, come in!"

"Don't want to interrupt you. I should have rung or something." Liar!

"No, no worries. Come in. I've been dying to talk to somebody." I wasn't sure I liked just being 'somebody', but walked on in. A familiar-sounding engine started turning over in a corner of the room.

"Shut up, Ham. It's Chris." Stacey turned back to me. "Hey, sit down. I'll make some coffee, eh?"

"Great, thanks. Why do you call him Ham?" I'd run out of rehearsed speeches but I did have an interest in this name.

Stacey limped across the small living room towards an even smaller kitchen. "Oh, because he's such a big fake. Mum christened him that — it's Ham like in 'hamming it up', you know? He always puts on this act of being fierce, but he's just a softie. Sugar?"

"No, thanks." The softie padded across to where I was sitting and dropped his chin on my knee in a "G'day" sort of way.

"I'm so glad you've come round. Mum was at work and then Polytech all day yesterday, and she had to go to work again this afternoon. She says office cleaning actually pays more than nursing. We might even be able to get another car — in about twenty years. Hey, would you mind coming to get your mug? I keep getting off-balance when I walk."

I eased out from under Ham's chin, went into the kitchen and picked up my mug of coffee. "How is the foot, anyway?" I asked.

"Oh, still a bit sore, but it's much better. Hey, thanks a lot for getting us home on Tuesday. Mum said it was really neat of you."

"Not a problem," I said as we sat down. Ham immediately plonked his chin on my knee again.

"He likes you," said Stacey.

"For breakfast or lunch?" I asked. She laughed and I felt us both relax.

The next half hour was great. We talked and talked. My coffee got cold. Stacey's a good listener — she understands what you're trying to say, and helps you over the embarrassing bits without making a fuss. I could tell she enjoys talking: she kept jumping around in her chair and tucking her legs under her, sometimes sitting on her sore foot and saying "Hell!" as she untucked her legs again. They really are nice legs.

We talked about Tae Kwan Do, of course. I told her about the mess I'd made at the last tournament. After I'd told her, I found it didn't really worry me any more. She said how much she was enjoying the club, and how good the people there were — "Especially the instructors," she grinned, and my stomach started to shiver again.

We talked about school, and how she got hacked off with people asking her why on earth she was taking Chemistry and Physics. "Because I'm quite good at them and I want to do lab work," she explained. We didn't talk about Kevin McAndrew.

Stacey had quite a lot to say about her mother — how she had to work really hard to bring Stacey up by herself. "There was this boyfriend she had when I was about twelve," Stacey said, "and he — he . . ." She trailed away and started biting her bottom lip, so I changed the subject back to Tae Kwan Do again. At the back of my mind, though, the comment about her Mum's boyfriend niggled.

I told her about my father, how he'd cleared out, and how things were now with Mum and Les and me. Stacey listened and nodded and smiled, and I felt as though I could be a friend to everyone, even McAndrew and Thatcher . . . well, almost.

Finally there was a bit of a silence. I think we were both feeling so good and relaxed. "Hey, would you like some more coffee?" Stacey asked, and I realised I hadn't drunk my first mug. I also realised what the time was.

"Oh hell, I'd better go!" I scrambled up out of my chair. Ham, who'd settled down by my feet, nudged my leg with his head and I almost fell over again. "Practice begins in an hour, and I haven't even started on the Urals."

Stacey looked puzzled. "Is that some sort of red belt pattern?" she asked, and laughed when I told her.

She limped across to the front door with me. "I'm coming to next Tuesday's practice," she said. "Even if I can't do the training, I'm gonna watch."

I had another brilliant idea. "Would you like me to show you some more of the patterns over the weekend?" I asked. "We can practise them in slow motion and it won't hurt your foot."

"That would be neat, Chris. Just ring or come round when you want to. Do you mind?"

Of course I didn't mind! I told her so.

There was another silence, and I suddenly realised how close together we were standing. She was holding Janelle's book. I noticed she had a spot starting, just beside her nose. Thank God she isn't perfect, I remember thinking.

Neither of us moved. I wanted to kiss her. Hell, I've got my hands in my pockets, I thought. I can't kiss a girl with my hands in my pockets! What am I going to do with them? And I'm still in my school uniform. And what'll I do if she hits me with the Tae Kwan Do book. Stacey was staring at me; she looked a bit anxious.

I took my hands out of my pockets, but don't remember where I put them. I leaned forward and kissed her, very gently.

Her mouth was soft and tasted slightly of coffee. She didn't move; just held her face still so that her lips stayed against mine.

After a couple of seconds I straightened up. "Sorry," I said. Oh well, I'll never be the world's greatest lover.

"It's all right," Stacey said. She looked . . . shy, I suppose. I kissed her again, just as gently, and this time there wasn't any doubt — she kissed me back. When I drew away again, Stacey's face was pink and I know mine was pinker. We looked at each other. Then "Yaaa-awwwnnn!" went Ham, who was watching us from the floor. We both burst out laughing.

"See ya, Stacey," I said.

"See ya, Chris," she said.

I ran all the way home, and said hello to everyone I met, even the dogs on the footpaths. I talked to Mum and Les, and I went to practice, and I must have done really well because Selwyn said "Good," three times, and I came home again, and I can hardly remember a single thing that happened.

I didn't get to sleep that night till after one o'clock. I lay there thinking how neat it had been kissing Stacey, and wondering when and where I could kiss her again. I wasn't worrying so much about the how, this time.

Something else probably helped keep me awake, too. I remembered that I still hadn't done a single thing about the industry of the Urals.

Chapter 10

When Josh rang me next morning before school to check on whether I'd be in next week's demonstration, I asked "What demonstration?" Obviously my mind hadn't been on Tae Kwan Do at the night before's practice.

Josh sighed. "Get your mother to look in your ear to see if your brain's fallen out."

Actually, I think I did remember Selwyn mentioning it. The local primary school were having their gala day Saturday week, and they were hoping some of our club would go along and do a demo for them.

Tae Kwan Do demonstrations are a bit of a giggle. You do all this flashy stuff that you hardly ever do any other time. Josh and Colin and I get about six of the others to kneel down in a row while we jump over them in a running side-kick, and smash a board that Selwyn's holding. Josh and Selwyn smash more boards with their elbows and fists. Little Brenda has a special routine I'll tell you about later. Like I say, it's mainly showing off, but it always gets people interested in joining the club. So I told Josh that, yeah, I'd be a starter.

I thought a bit about the demonstration while I walked to school. I thought a smaller bit about the industry of the Urals. I made myself think about them, since of course the only thing I really wanted to think about was Stacey.

I'm going to be private about it. I won't go writing STACEY 'N' CHRIS 4 EVA on desktops. And I won't do what I did in form two — sneak into the girls' loo during lesson time, and scribble the name of a girl I liked on the loo wall. The teachers thought she'd written it herself, and she got in trouble.

Anyway, let's be honest; I really don't know how keen Stacey is on me. Okay, she certainly kissed me back the second time yesterday, but maybe that was just because she didn't know what else to do. If I tried it again she might laugh at me, which would be a real shrink. Something like that happened with a different girl last year, and I wanted to crawl under the carpet.

There was a bit of a problem in PE. Mrs Jennings let the guys get the weights out, and a few of them started showing off for the girls. No prizes for guessing that McAndrew was one of the few. They haven't got a clue, most of them — they think the idea of weight-training is to stick as much as you can on the bar and still get it above your head. The real point is the number of repetitions you can do to build up your stamina.

I wasn't interested in doing any weight work today. Friday's usually my day off from training — you need that to keep you fresh. I was perfectly happy playing badminton at one end of the gym with a couple of other guys. But McAndrew couldn't leave things alone. "Hey, Atkinson!" he called. "Aren't you gonna show us how it's done? Can't you do anything without your little white pyjamas?"

I couldn't be bothered making a thing of it. "Doesn't turn me on," I said, without turning round.

"Oooooh, doesn't turn him on!" said Thatcher. "You'll have to tell Stacey that."

They were working up to something, those guys, so I kept a low profile; I'm not interested in any aggro.

I wished Stacey had been at school so I could just say hi to her. I'd decided I wasn't going to go round to her place again before Saturday; that would be too pushy. But I was going to ring her up after school.

I rang her as soon as I got into the house. Well, Mum would be back from work soon and might want the phone, or a museum might ring up Les and make an offer for his car. And anyway, if I waited and thought about it, my stomach would get so shivery that I wouldn't be able to talk properly.

The phone was picked up at the other end, and Stacey's voice said "Hello?"

"Hi, Stacey." (I'd rehearsed this opening speech, too.) "It's—"

"Oh hi, Chris. I was just thinking about you." She was just thinking about me! I made my free hand into a fist and punched it two or three times in the air.

"How are you?" I asked. "How's the foot?"

"Oh, fine. How are you?"

"Oh, fine." This was becoming a conversation that Shakespeare would not have been proud of writing. "Would you still like to try a few training patterns tomorrow, like we were talking about?"

"Yeah, sure. You don't mind coming round?"

I told Stacey James that I didn't mind coming round. I suggested that perhaps I, Chris Atkinson, could arrive about eleven o'clock in the morning if that was all right with Stacey James. That was all right with Stacey James.

I said goodbye. I replaced the receiver and stared at the sweaty mark where my hand had been holding it. I thought about all the other friendly, witty things I'd planned to say and had forgotten.

I expected Friday night to be pretty boring. It often is. You know, you spend the week looking forward to the end of school, and then it's all a bit tame when it comes.

But this Friday, before they went out to the pub with Les's mates, Mum and Les got into one of their discussions. They call them discussions; I call them arguments. It usually happens when Les has read something in the paper or seen something on TV that he disagrees with, and he starts sounding off about it to anyone who's round. Funny — he gets steamed up about other people, but not about himself.

This time he was on about a news report how some high school somewhere wouldn't let a pregnant seventh form girl stay on at the school after her pregnancy started to show. The girl wanted to stay and sit her exams. Her parents wanted her to as well, but the school's Board of Trustees or whatever weren't having it.

"How about the father of the baby?" Les was saying. "What if he's a seventh former too? I bet he doesn't have to leave school!"

"Oh come on, Les!" Mum was saying. "It must be difficult for the teachers and the other kids."

"Why?" Les was getting more and more worked up. "It's not their fault! Good lead-in for some healthy sex education."

The discussion went on for a bit, then he and Mum started laughing and pretending to punch each other. Afterwards, Les went off to make a cup of tea and things quietened down. I felt almost disappointed.

On Saturday morning, I told Mum I was going to help someone from Tae Kwan Do with their training. Mum said, "Fine, love. Just leave some hot water when you shower this time, won't you?"

"And give our regards to Stacey and her mum," Les added. Smart sods.

I walked round to Stacey's place. Like I said, it doesn't look cool to arrive on a bike. Anyway, I wanted time to work out some suave conversation. There was heavy metal pounding away from the front flat once again, and a couple of guys with tattoos all over their arms were carrying cartons of empty beer bottles out of it. They gave me a nod.

Stacey's mum answered the door, helped by Ham, who was letting the whole street know that someone had knocked. He sniffed my knees and trod on my foot.

"Hello, Chris," said Mrs James. "Stacey said you'd been to see her the other day."

I could hear the coolness in her voice. "Hi, Mrs James. Yeah, sorry — I should have rung first, but I was on my way home from school."

"No, that's fine," Mrs James said, and smiled. "It's just that, you know, a girl in the flat by herself, and some of the things you hear about . . . well, you have to be careful. That's partly why we got Ham."

"Yeah, fair enough," I said.

Stacey was wearing her track pants and a white T-shirt carrying the message WOMENPOWER RULES. Fine by me, I thought.

"Hi," she said.

"Hi," I said right back. We grinned at each other.

"Where would you like to practise, Chris?" Mrs James asked. "Stacey said you might want to kick all our washing off the line — is that right?"

I laughed. "Not this time, Mrs James. Not with

Stacey's sore foot. I thought we'd just do some more blocking and punching patterns, since she learned the first ones so fast."

Stacey took me outside, onto a concrete yard area next to their flat, and we started straightaway. I think we were both glad to have something to do. I was feeling a bit embarrassed after Thursday, and I wasn't sure what to say. Tae Kwan Do helped.

Stacey learned the new patterns and blocks just as fast as she'd learned the first ones. She's a natural; she should really impress Master Kim when her first grading comes round. She chewed away at her bottom lip, and the time flew past.

Three interesting things happened. First, I looked up once and saw Mrs James at the window, watching Stacey. She had this really proud expression on her face. When she caught my eye she gave a smile and a wave, but kept watching for a while.

Second — Ham was watching too. The first time I reached out my hand to change the position of Stacey's elbow, I heard the engine rev up and saw Ham get to his feet. "It's all right, Ham," said Stacey, and he sat down again, but each time I touched Stacey he would rumble for a second. "You don't need Tae Kwan Do," I told her. "You've got Ham Can Do." She stuck her tongue out at me again.

The third thing? About halfway through, I held Stacey's hand so that she could keep her balance with her sore foot while she learned how to lift her knee up to block low crescent kicks. After she'd finished practising the move and didn't need to balance any more, I realised we were still holding hands. Ham gave another rumble and we let go, but I felt great.

When we went back inside, Mrs James was clearing a whole lot of study books off the living-room table.

"Chris," she said. "I'd ask you to stay for some coffee, but Stacey's helping me with my office-cleaning this afternoon, and I have to start straight after lunch." I made polite noises.

"How's the study going, Mum?" Stacey asked. "Mum's going to sit her Charge Nurse's exam in a couple of months," she told me. "She studies more than I do — though that's not hard!"

"They say it'll give me greater job prospects," Mrs James said. "Then they tell me not to hold my breath. You don't know what to believe. Anyhow, how's Stacey getting on with the Tae Kwan Do?"

"Really excellent," I said. "She does everything right and really pays attention."

Mrs James gave Stacey another proud smile, and smiled at me, too. "Well, from what she's been saying, her instructor's worth paying attention to."

I felt myself go red.

Later, on the way home, it occurred to me that Mrs James had probably been talking about Selwyn, and I felt myself go red again.

Chapter 11

I was feeling so good that I worked on the industry of the Urals for a couple of hours on Saturday afternoon. Usually I prefer to save my energy for more important things, like . . . um . . . er . . . Maybe Stacey's having a good effect on me?

Anyway, you'll be as rapt as I was to learn that the Urals produce 30% of Europe's pig-iron. Like I said, I always thought it was ham you got from pigs.

Les spent most of Saturday out in the garage amputating bits of his car. I reckon he stayed out there because whenever he comes inside, Mum wants to know if he's had any luck with job enquiries.

Even after the Urals I still felt good, so I went out to the garage and asked if he wanted a hand.

Les gave me a look that was surprised and knowing at the same time. "Had a pleasant morning, did you?" he asked.

"Dunno what you're talking about," I told him.

"Just thought you'd need skilled help with the car repairing. What part do you want me to kick first?"

I was the one who had the last word for a change.

Sunday was a flat day. I went for quite a long run that took me past the supermarket a couple of times. After all, Mrs James might be needing a hand with her groceries again — except they didn't have a car any longer, of course. There wasn't any sign of her, anyway; just a grey, gritty carpark under a grey, gritty sky.

I kept wishing I could ring up Stacey, just to say hello, ask her how her foot was, would she be back to school on Monday, had she really meant to hold my hand the way she had on Saturday . . . those sorts of little things. But I didn't feel brave enough, and I don't want Mrs James to think I'm being a nuisance. I could tell from the way she looks at Stacey that she'd do anything to protect her if she thought she needed to.

I kept telling myself on the run that I had to concentrate. There were less than two weeks till grading. There was next Saturday's Demonstration, too, and the tournament. I was supposed to be keeping my mind focused on them. Trouble was, my mind kept deciding to focus itself on Stacey.

I spent Sunday evening getting more and more depressed about things. Finally, when Les asked me didn't I have anyone to coach for Tae Kwan Do tonight, I lost my cool.

"No, I haven't!" I snapped. "And I'm sick of listening to your pathetic jokes!"

"Chris! Don't you talk to Les like that!" Mum snapped right back. "You apologise!"

"It's all right—" Les started to say.

"It is not all right!" Mum interrupted. "You're too easy on people, Les. I have to run everything around here!"

Next thing I knew, the two of them were off on what they'd call a discussion. "Sorry," I mumbled in the direction of Les. Neither he nor Mum heard me; they were too busy hearing each other.

"I'm going to bed," I announced. They didn't take any notice.

I intercepted Les the next morning as he was sneaking out to the garage. "Sorry about last night, Les," I said. "I should've zipped my lip."

"No worries," Les grinned. "Tell you what — next time reach out with the other hand and zip mine, too."

I rolled my eyes when his back was turned. I guess he'll never change.

Then it was Mum's turn to intercept me. "You know, don't you, Chris," she began "that you're welcome to invite anyone from Tae Kwan Do or school round here any time you want — provided it's okay with their parents. You're a fifth former after all. Les and I are out quite a bit, but we know you're sensible."

I realised Mum was giving me a coded message. I felt pleased that she trusted me; especially since I'd heard her tell Les once that after the way my father behaved with other women, she thought she'd never trust any male again. I guess that's why she keeps fussing over me and my friends.

I saw Stacey first thing at school. I do like starting the week off on a good note! She still limped a bit, but she looked fine — as I believe I may have said before? Even in our school's glamorous grey uniform she seems all sparkly to me.

"I've got heaps of work to catch up," she groaned. "Biology and Chemistry. And Maths!"

"If there's anything you need to know about the chemistry of the Urals, just ask me," I told her.

"Janelle says there's a Tae Kwan Do demonstration at the primary school next Saturday," Stacey went on. "Do we have to learn anything for that?"

"No — actually, yes!" I changed direction fast, because another brilliant idea was suddenly yelling and waving inside my mind. "There are a few special moves you have to do. Hey, do you want to come round to our place on the way to the club tomorrow? I can explain them to you then, if you like."

"Okay," she agreed. "If you don't mi—"

"I don't mind!" I jumped in.

Stacey laughed. "I'd better go and see about Chemistry," she said, and headed off.

After I'd done my weight-training and clothesline-kicking that evening, I looked at myself for a while in the bathroom mirror. I wish I wasn't so skinny; I'm quite strong and wiry-looking in my arms and legs, but you can count every one of my ribs, and my collarbones look as if I'm wearing a coat-hanger under my skin. Last year I was going to send away for one of those 'I Can Give You a Body That Will Make Women Dribble' type of courses, but Mum said not to be silly. "You've got a lovely teenage boy's shape," she said.

Nice of her to say so, but can a guy really trust his mum? I just hope it's not muscles that Stacey's keen on; if she ever sees me with my shirt off, she'll run screaming back to Kevin McAndrew.

I wondered if I should tell Mum about Stacey coming round after school tomorrow, but decided not to. After all, she said she trusts me.

Only one important thing happened at school on Tuesday, apart from getting 11 out of 20 for the Urals, which was good for me, and being given an English assignment on Television Reviewing, which wasn't good for me. Stacey said, "Can I come round about half-past four to learn those moves? If you don't mind?"

"Yes you can, and no I don't." It was one of my better replies, and it got me a giggle.

I had a shower as soon as I got home. Since Mum was at work, and Les was spending most of the day at a mate's trying to Sellotape his gearbox back together, I was the only one home. Then I wandered around feeling nervous, starting to sweat again, and practising saying, "Would you like a cup of coffee? Would you like a cup of coffee?" in my coolest voice.

The doorbell rang at 4.28. Stacey stood on the doorstep in her gi, carrying a big red and black cardigan.

"Have you looked at that weird English assignment yet?" she asked as we walked through to the living room.

"Would you like a coff of cuppee?" I asked.

We both stopped and stood looking at each other. "What did you say?" Stacey asked, and began to grin.

"Would you like a cuff of cop— oh hell!" I put my hands on her shoulders and kissed her.

She jerked a bit, so I ended up kissing her mainly on the corner of her mouth. But she moved her lips to the right place and it was the same as when I kissed her the first time, except that this time she tasted of toothpaste. When I lifted my head up, I realised she'd put one arm around me. The other one was still holding her cardigan.

I could feel my heart banging. Stacey was staring at me, and I could see a shape that I supposed was me, reflected in her pupils. As I bent to kiss her again, she closed her eyes and turned her face up further towards me.

I must have moved forward, because I could feel her body against mine. She flinched away, just for a second. Then she relaxed and leaned towards me. My hands were behind her back. I could feel the cool cotton of her gi, and I could feel her, warm under the gi. Fancy kissing someone in a Tae Kwan Do uniform, the voice in my head was saying.

After the second kiss, we stayed standing with our arms around each other. Well, with three of our arms around each other. Stacey was still holding her cardigan; I wondered if I should tell her that our living room floor was quite clean, and it would be okay if she dropped the cardigan.

"I thought you were going to show me some moves," Stacey said.

"I just did," I replied. Cheap line, but I couldn't resist it.

Stacey laughed, and I felt her body shake a little bit where it was pressed against me. Of course that made me shiver, from my shoulders right down to my knees.

We didn't say anything for a while; just stood there holding each other. After a few seconds I heard the cardigan drop on the carpet, and Stacey's other arm came around behind me. She must have agreed that our living room floor was clean.

"You're quite tall, aren't you?" she said suddenly.

"Compared to what?" I asked.

"Well, compared to me," she said.

"Just as well, eh, Shorty?" I felt really good and confident now. "Might be a bit weird if I had to stand on tippy-toes to kiss you."

Stacey laughed again. Then she looked up at me and her face went serious. I kissed her a third time. Mint toothpaste, I decided.

"Do you know what I'd like?" she said after that.

Oh man! I thought. "What?" I gurgled.

"A cuff of coppee," she grinned.

Stacey sat down and I made two mugs of finest instant coffee while we agreed we couldn't make any sense out of our TV reviewing assignment. I sat down in the chair next to her and gave her the mug without the chip in it. Mum would've been proud of me.

"Nice coppee," she said, and grinned again.

We talked just like we had at her place last Thursday, about school, and other kids, and mothers, and the guys with the tats in the end flat at her place. ("They're quite nice, really," Stacey said. "They call Mum and me both 'Lady'."), and about Tae Kwan Do and what an amazing instructor Selwyn is.

After a while, Stacey put her empty coffee mug down on the floor beside her, and I reached across and held her hand.

"Last time you did that, Ham started growling," Stacey said.

"Yeah," I agreed. "But this—"

There was a scraping noise at the front door. A key turned, the door opened, and Mum walked in.

Stacey and I both jumped up, which was probably the worst thing we could have done. I had this sudden flashback to when I was about five, and Mum

101

caught me and the girl from across the road playing doctors in our garage. (It had been the girl's idea, of course.)

Mum looked at Stacey and me, at the coffee mugs, at Stacey's cardigan still lying in the middle of the floor, and I could see her start to wonder.

"Hello, love. Hello, Stacey," she said, very politely.

"Hi, Mum."

"Hi, Mrs Atkinson."

"Stacey came round so I could tell her about the Tae Kwan Do demonstration on Saturday," I explained, talking faster than I needed to.

"I see," said Mum, which meant that she didn't. She looked at her watch. "You'd better be getting ready for practice, Chris. It's nearly quarter to."

Hell, I thought, we must have been talking for an hour! I tore into my room and changed into my gi. When I came back out, Stacey and Mum were in the kitchen, chatting and laughing, which made me feel a lot better. But Mum still gave me a bit of a look as we left.

"Didn't you tell your mother I was coming round?" Stacey asked as we walked down the footpath.

"No," I mumbled. "Sorry."

Stacey said nothing. We went round a corner and turned into the pedestrian walkway that's a short-cut to a street near the club. There's one of those galvanised-pipe barriers at the walkway entrance to stop maniacs on motorbikes tearing through. I stood aside to let Stacey go through first, and her hand touched mine. We went on down the walkway and out into the next street holding hands, but saying nothing. Just as we got out into the street, there was a whirr of bike wheels behind us, and Leon shot past. "Hey, lovers!" he yelled. "Wait till I tell Kevin McAndrew, Stacey!"

"Cheeky little turd!" called Stacey. Her face had gone pink, but she was still holding my hand.

I worked hard at practice that night. I wanted to show everyone that I was still thinking about grading and tournament. I even forgot about Stacey a few times; then I'd look over and see her training with the other white belts, her pony tail bobbing up and down, moving carefully on her sore foot, and remember the taste of mint toothpaste.

Before we split into groups according to our belts, Selwyn took the whole club through every pattern from white belt through yellow, green, blue and red. It's a really interesting idea; it makes the senior belts work on the basics, and even though the white and yellow belts can only do bits of the more advanced patterns, it gives them an appreciation of the sorts of things they'll learn later on.

We did our warm-down exercises, bowed to Selwyn and said goodnight. I wondered if maybe Stacey might be able to walk part of the way home with me, but when we came out of the hall, Mrs James and Ham were waiting.

"Hi, Mrs James. Hi, Ham," I said. I got a smile from one and a panting noise from the other. I must be making progress, I thought. So I hurried on. "Stacey should be fine for the demo on Saturday, Mrs James," I chirped. "I explained it all to her when she came round this afternoon."

Before I finished, I knew something wasn't right. Stacey was silent beside me, and Mrs James was looking at her, not at me.

"I didn't know you were going to Chris's place this afternoon?" Mrs James said to Stacey. Stacey said something I didn't catch.

"Well, we'd better be on our way," said Mrs James. She turned and started off along the footpath. Ham gave me a short growl and started off with her.

Stacey began to follow them. "Didn't you tell your mum you were coming round either?" I asked her, as quietly as I could.

She gave me an embarrassed look. "No," she mumbled. "Sorry."

I watched as she hurried to catch up with her mother. Mothers 2, Kids 0.

Chapter 12

"Both eyes," Selwyn says sometimes at training. "Both eyes." It's his way of telling you to face up to your opponent or a training problem, fair and square. As soon as I got home, I went into the kitchen and faced up to Mum. Les must have realised I wanted to have a private talk with her and pretended he needed something in the living room.

"Sorry I didn't tell you Stacey was coming round, Mum," I said. "I just didn't think of it. (Ahem) She wanted to know about the demonstration we're giving — the one at the primary school this Saturday."

Mum nodded. "That's good, love," she said. "Like I say, I know we can trust you, but it could make things a bit easier if you tell us. Saves embarrassment."

I thought of the guilty way Stacey and I had jumped up when Mum came in, and I knew what she meant.

"Did Mrs James know Stacey was coming here?" Mum asked.

"Er — no, I don't think she did, actually." Well, it wasn't not the truth.

"Might be an idea to explain to her," Mum suggested. "Les says she's inclined to worry a bit."

I thought that sounded pretty rich, coming from Les! Then I thought 'both eyes' to myself again, and went through to the living room to use the phone. Now poor old Les had to pretend there was something he wanted back in the kitchen.

"Mrs James?" I said. "It's Chris Atkinson here." I felt the temperature at the other end of the phone drop four degrees.

"Mrs James, I invited Stacey round here this afternoon. She asked about Saturday's demonstration, so I offered to show her what she had to do." The voice at the other end of the phone lost a degree of ice, so I went on. "I'm sorry if it caused any hassles. I didn't mean to go behind your back or anything."

It sounded like greasing to me, but Mrs James' voice was almost sunny when she spoke.

"Thanks, Chris. I usually ask Stacey to let me know if she's going out by herself. It's just that . . . well, anyway, as long as she remembers next time. Would you like to talk to her? She's just doing something horrible to her dinner with tomato sauce."

"No, it's okay thanks, Mrs James. Just tell her to eat plenty of protein – she'll need it for Saturday's demo." I hung up. Then wished I had asked to talk to Stacey. And then felt pleased I hadn't been pushy.

Had Stacey not told her mother she was coming to see me in case her mother said no? Did that mean she'd wanted to come and see me? I squeezed my head with my hands, to bring it back down to normal size. Then I went and tried to make sense out of our English assignment on TV reviewing. After twenty minutes of that, I felt my head — or my brain, at any rate — was down to half its normal size.

I thought about Stacey for ages after I'd gone to bed. Things she said, how good she is at Tae Kwan Do, how she'd held my hand. I tried to concentrate on other things, like planning my patterns for the grading — just over a week away now. But instead, I found I was planning how to kiss Stacey next time I had the chance. Finally I had to get up and make my bed all over again.

Wednesday morning at school, I came through the double doors into the corridor at the same time as Kevin McAndrew. Hello, hello, I thought. "G'day," I said.

I expected him to say, "Piss off," or "Up yours, Atkinson," or even just ignore me. Instead he asked, "You done anything with that English assignment yet?"

"Yeah," I replied. "I've spilled a cup of coffee all over it." Not true, actually, but clever I thought.

McAndrew gave what was nearly a laugh. "Might

try that on mine," he said. He's a different guy when he's not with Thatcher.

There's another side to that, of course — the sort of guy he becomes when he is with Thatcher. I saw the two of them hanging around the back of the assembly hall at morning interval, talking to Leon. Like I say, Leon's altogether too impressed by these macho guys. Since he was the one who'd seen Stacey and me holding hands on the way to Tae Kwan Do last night, I hoped he was keeping his mouth shut.

Come PE, I knew that he hadn't. Mrs Jennings had us playing tag. It probably sounds silly, a fifth form class doing that, but it's quite fun when you get started. Good for the reflexes, too.

This was the sort of tag where everyone who's caught joins the other chasers, and nobody is allowed off the gym floor. Stacey wasn't playing; she's still being careful with her foot. But McAndrew and Thatcher were, and I had this feeling it might pay me to watch my back.

Soon there were only about six of us left untagged. I was jogging around, avoiding three or four guys who were aiming to work me into a corner.

Suddenly one of them looked startled and called "Watch it!" I turned round fast, and there were Thatcher and McAndrew coming at me. They were gripping each other's wrists so their arms made a bar at about chest height. If they hit me like that, I'd end up spread across the floor.

Without thinking, I went straight into a back

stance with my right arm in a block position. Their linked hands hit my arm and were jerked apart. I was braced in the stance and hardly moved, but they staggered about all over the place.

There were a few cheers from the kids who'd seen it. Thatcher and McAndrew glared at me. "Okay, I'm tagged," I said, and walked away. That's what Selwyn would expect me to do.

Every time Stacey and I saw each other at school, we'd stop and talk. She'd look kind of shy and I'd feel a bit the same. She was looking forward to the demonstration "if I can get my homework done first," she added. She'd been spending lunchtimes catching up on what she missed when she was away. She's got determination, all right.

So have McAndrew and Thatcher, in a different way. On Thursday, the day after that business in the gym, I was walking as slowly as I could to History after lunch when the footsteps I'd heard coming up behind me suddenly got faster, and a shoulder thumped against me. I stumbled sideways, got my foot caught in a bag some fool had left lying there, and fell onto my hands and knees.

"Oh dear! So sorry!" sneered Thatcher as he and McAndrew went on down the corridor. I followed even more slowly, reminding myself of Selwyn again.

He — Selwyn — gave us a relaxing practice on Thursday. Tae Kwan Do can be fun as well as training, and since the demonstration was only two days away we worked out routines for that and then played speed games — how many kicks and punches you can land on a bag in twenty seconds (I won); how far you can knock the bag (Josh and Colin tied); how many kicks and punches you can do at the same time (Wiri won, but then he's got an unfair number of arms and legs).

We even played tag, but not the way McAndrew and Thatcher do. I wouldn't have been surprised if crafty old Selwyn had got me to chase Stacey, but as her foot was starting to hurt a bit he made her sit down. Instead we all had to tag Janelle. Easier said than done — the kid's like an eel.

Everyone enjoyed themselves. Leon pretended to think it was all a bit childish, but he got keen, too, when Selwyn put him in the board-breaking group for Saturday. Selwyn knows just how to handle Leon.

It was a special practice in another way, too. Frances' baby was due very soon, so she was giving up training for a bit. Trish — Wiri's mum — had bought her a pair of white baby's pants and a little white top. She'd sewn a miniature black belt and some club badges onto the clothes, and they looked hilarious. Frances couldn't stop laughing when Trish presented them to her.

Mrs James and Ham were waiting outside at the end of practice. Both eyes, I told myself. "Hi, Mrs James," I said. "Hi, Ham James."

Mrs James laughed. Like I said before, when she

smiles or laughs, she looks a totally different person. "Hello, Chris," she said. Then "Hello, Stacey," with a proud smile as a certain white belt appeared. And then, out of the blue, "You coming in our direction, Chris?"

Hell yes, of course I was — even if I had to walk an extra ten blocks to get home after! So for quarter of an hour we three humans walked along the footpath together, while Ham trotted ahead and embarrassed us against lamp-posts. I was on my very best behaviour, because I sensed that Mrs James was checking me out.

Chapter 13

Saturday morning. Demonstration day at the primary school gala. A week till grading. Seven weeks till tournament. Three weeks till the end of term. There's my priorities in four nutshells.

I ironed my gi — then found I'd ironed the pants so that the creases were down the sides of the legs, and I had to do it again. I had a shower while Les made heavy jokes about how the hot water bill had gone up in the last month. I put on my gi and a tracksuit top and headed off for the primary school. Les said that if I waited quarter of an hour I could get a lift in the car with him and Mum. I said thanks, but I wanted to be sure of getting there on time and alive. Mum gave me a bit of a look, so I grinned to show I was being friendly.

Even at my advanced age, I like school galas. I like to hunt around the bookstall for any decent horror comics, and if I've got any extra money I pig out on the sausage sizzle. I didn't have any money today, extra or otherwise, but Josh shouted me a sausage anyway.

I was looking for just one person. I recognised the red and black cardigan first. I could see it clearly because Stacey was with her mother and Ham, and people were making sure they left a clear space around Ham. I watched Stacey until they disappeared around a corner.

The Tae Kwan Do demo started at eleven o'clock. We met around the back of the school's assembly hall, and gave our tracksuit tops and jackets and cardigans to Frances to look after. Then we formed two lines and jogged around onto the concrete playground where we were going to do our showing off.

We looked pretty good, actually. Selwyn always tells us we have a responsibility to give 100% at everything; it's a way of showing respect for the discipline of Tae Kwan Do. So we didn't muck about.

Firstly we went through the most basic pattern, the punches and kicks and blocks that all white belts learn. The pattern ends with a front punch and a yell, so nineteen fists all snapped forward and nineteen voices yelled "Tae Kwan!" at the same time. You could hear the echoes bounce off the assembly hall wall. And you could hear Ham's echo bounce back as he replied, "Boom! Boom!"

Then we did our fancy bits. Janelle showed how

you can flatten a big guy like Colin the truck driver in about five seconds. She may have done it more thoroughly than she meant to, because when Colin got up he was rubbing his backside thoughtfully. Josh and I did some free-sparring — limited contact stuff where you only land kicks and punches lightly but do everything as fast as you can.

Following this came one of my favourite bits, when Selwyn did some free-sparring with Brenda. Brenda is only eight or nine years old, and she's been in the club for about a year now. She only comes up to Selwyn's waist, and the kids in the club call her Atom Ant.

Anyway, Selwyn got down on his knees on the concrete and shuffled around like that. The crowd laughed and cheered, especially when Selwyn pretended to be knocked over.

Next, six of the yellow belts and green belts knelt down in a row on the concrete. Josh and I took a run, leaped over them, and broke the board that Selwyn was holding at the other end. Josh does this with a reverse kick, which is really impressive. He's a red belt black tab, after all. I broke mine with a punch, but it still must have looked okay because there was a lot of clapping. I could see Stacey sitting with the other white belts and clapping too. I didn't mind at all.

I'll tell you a secret about breaking boards. It's easy. As long as the wood is dry and the grain is all running one way, and as long as someone's holding

114

the board really firmly, there's nothing to it. Nothing much, anyway. What you have to do is punch or kick straight through the thing — tell yourself that you're going to strike right through to the far side, and don't hold back. If you do it half-heartedly, that's when the board doesn't get broken and you get bruised.

Some movies make a real macho thing out of board-breaking. You see people punching holes in roof tiles, smashing bottles or big blocks of ice, breaking bricks with a head-butt — that sort of stuff. I saw one movie where a guy broke a baseball bat with a shin kick!

Selwyn reckons that's crap — Tae Kwan Do is about self-control, not self-display. He won't let the junior belts do any board-breaking, and he won't let anyone else try it till they've done lots of punch-bag work to toughen their hands and feet.

This day he got Janelle to break one board with a punch. It was the first time she'd tried it outside the club and you could tell she was nervous, but she went for it flat out and it broke cleanly. Later on I saw her showing off her skinned knuckles to her mates.

Colin broke two boards held together. He's strong, all right. Then Selwyn broke one board — but it was one that he got Josh to toss in the air, and he smacked it with a jumping spinning reverse kick while it was still falling! That's really amazing: it's much harder to break a board when nobody's holding it. It has to be really quick — you've got to kick right through it before your foot can push it away, if you see what I mean.

Finally, six of us lined up in a row. A couple of yellow or white belts stood opposite each of us holding a board, and we each smashed our board with a different kick or punch. This always looks spectacular, too – a row of boards splitting one after the other.

By what I don't believe was coincidence, Selwyn got Stacey to hold my board with Wiri. Wiri had an enormous grin on his face, while Stacey's eyes were huge as I came at the board. I have to admit I put on a tough expression that I didn't need, and made a big thing out of the punch. When I saw the knowing look on Selwyn's face I felt suitably embarrassed.

The boards split *clack! clack! clack! clack! clack!* Josh, me, Trish, Colin, Janelle. Leon last . . . and his board didn't break.

I saw what happened. He tried for a spinning snap kick like Selwyn had done to his board earlier. It's a hard move for anyone under a blue belt to do, but it looks cool. That's why Leon tried it. But he wasn't properly balanced when his foot hit the board, so it didn't break.

"Punch," said Selwyn quietly.

Leon either didn't hear or didn't take any notice. He tried another spinning snap kick, but he was angry now and wasn't concentrating enough. His foot thumped the board a second time. Little Brenda and the other white belt who were gripping the board

116

staggered, but still it didn't break. There was a sympathetic murmur from the crowd.

Then someone yelled, "More Weetbix, eh kid?" and I recognised Dwayne Thatcher's voice. Nobody laughed, but Leon's face went tight and furious.

"Punch," said Selwyn again. This time Leon heard him. He went for the simplest move — a forward reverse punch. It should have split the board easily, but Leon's timing and confidence were shot. There was another loud thump. Leon himself winced and staggered, but the board stayed put.

"Stop," Selwyn told him in the same quiet voice. Then he turned to the crowd, said "Thank you for your attention, ladies and gentlemen," and gave them a perfect Tae Kwan Do bow.

Everyone started clapping and we jogged back behind the hall to get our jackets from Frances. She had three or four of them piled on her pregnant stomach, including mine. I didn't know where to look while I took it.

Leon didn't know where to look, either. He wouldn't talk to anyone; just snatched his jacket and walked away. Wiri called, "Hey, Leon! Don't you want your Coke?" The primary school had provided a couple of cartons of Coke for us.

"Stick your Coke," Leon grunted, and kept going. Trish and Colin and Frances looked at one another and shook their heads.

I ended up next to Stacey as we got our Cokes. It was accidental, of course — I only needed to squeeze

117

past Josh and two others. I'd planned to say, "Want to come and have a look at the book stall?" but Stacey got in first.

"Want to come and have a look at the book stall?" she said.

"Yeah, why not?" I agreed, trying to sound as if I didn't even know there was a book stall at the gala.

The first thing I saw in the classroom where they were selling all the books and magazines was a pile of old Judge Dredd comics. Okay, they're gross, but I'm a real fan of them. I was just about to reach out when a hand shot in front of me.

"Oh, neat! Judge Dredd!" exclaimed Stacey, while I gawped at her. "Mum can't stand these, but I love them. And I've even got some money from helping her clean those offices." Next thing I knew, Stacey had a pile of magazines under her arm, she'd paid the woman in charge, and we were leaving the room.

"Nothing there you wanted, Chris?"

"Ah — no, no." My brain was still trying to catch up to what had happened. "Shall I carry those for you?" I offered. Stacey passed me the comics, then slipped her hand into my non-magazine-holding one. We strolled on across the playground like that while I ordered my stomach to stop shivering. It disobeyed.

Stacey doesn't wriggle her hand around or let it flop inside yours like a sick fish the way some girls in my vast experience do. She just holds mine without any fuss.

We passed Colin and Selwyn with their families in

front of the Drown-the-Clown stall and got some grins, plus a huge wink from Colin. We passed Janelle and her mates by the Crazy Heads. Very appropriate place to find them. They all nudged one another and giggled. Typical.

As we rounded the corner of a prefab we saw Dwayne Thatcher and Leon sitting on a seat, both smoking. (Don't sneer, Atkinson: your own tobacco times went light up, suck up, throw up!) Leon gave us a 'stuff you' kind of stare but looked uncomfortable. Thatcher said, "Thought you had better taste, Stacey."

Stacey snapped, "You wouldn't know good taste if it bit you on the bum, Thatcher." She held my hand even tighter and we went on around the other side of the prefab.

And there were four familiar faces. Three of them were deep in conversation, the fourth had its mouth open and its tongue hanging out. The moment it saw Stacey and me it trotted over and sniffed at our joined hands. Maybe it thought we might be carrying a dinosaur's shinbone for its lunch.

When I saw Mrs James, I started to let go of Stacey's hand, but she gripped mine tighter still. "Hi, Mum, Mrs Atkinson, Les," she said. It sounded a bit like a roll call.

Mum and Les just smiled at us and started saying how much they'd enjoyed the demo, how quickly Stacey was learning (that made Mrs James look pleased), how I might be good at breaking boards but they could never get me to chop the firewood. Mind you, Mum and Les were holding hands themselves. Mum was really relaxed. Sometimes Les's easy-going ways rub off on her; sometimes they rub her up the wrong way. Today things were fine.

I think Mrs James wasn't quite sure what to say at first; she looked sort of worried for a second. But then she smiled and chatted away, too. She's quite pretty for thirty-two or thirty-three. I could see the resemblance between her and Stacey.

"I suppose we'd better be on our way," Mrs James said after a while. "It must be nearly lunchtime." Ham was lying on his side on the warm concrete by now. And on my foot. I tried to move it once, but he made one of his engine-revving noises, so I left my foot where it was, losing circulation.

"Why don't you come and have lunch at our place?" Mum suddenly said. "You and Stacey. It's just French bread and things, but we've got plenty."

Les agreed immediately, and I realised he knows how much such things matter to Mum. "Yes, come on, Karen. You can explain last week's computer assignment to me — the one where I ended up losing eight million dollars."

Mrs James looked a bit uncertain. "Well . . ." She looked at Stacey, then at Mum. "If you're sure it's no trouble . . ." she began.

"No trouble at all," Mum and Les both said at the same time, and we all laughed.

"Oh, but what about Ham?" Mrs James asked.

"No ham, but there's lots of French bread," joked Les. Stacey and Mum and I groaned. Ham opened one eye and snarled at Les, which was what he deserved.

"Ham can walk home with Chris and Stacey," Mum said. "We senior citizens can go in the car."

"If you're going in Les's car, we'll probably get home before you do," I told Mrs James.

"The cheek of children nowadays!" Les shook his head and winked at me as the three of them moved off towards the carpark. The three of us — Stacey, Ham and me — moved off towards the school drive. Halfway along it we met Thatcher again. He looked at Ham and didn't make any smart cracks this time.

Stacey and I didn't say much on the way to our place. I was walking in a sort of contented silence. I had something I wanted to say before we reached home, though. I rehearsed it inside my head several times to get the words right. Finally I blurted it out as we detoured around Ham, who was investigating a nasty-looking pile on the grass verge.

"You're a pretty special female, Shorty James," I told her.

She stopped still and I almost fell over Ham, who gave a disapproving rumble. Stacey was staring at the footpath. Oh hell, I thought, I've said the wrong thing again.

"I feel safe with you," Stacey said. We walked on.

"Hey!" I said suddenly. "I hope the olds haven't started on the French bread. I'm starving!"

Chapter 14

The week following the demonstration was pretty quiet. A calm week, I suppose you could call it.

McAndrew and Thatcher kept giving me dirty looks in the corridors, and I kept watching my back as I went down those corridors, but nothing happened.

My English assignment on television reviewing didn't draw a very big audience (ha, ha). I wrote a History essay on 'Women's Expectations in the 20th Century' and spelled 'expectations' wrong every time.

There was some sort of argument going on about possible Human Relationships lessons for fifth formers. Since everyone knows that human relationships really means — you know — s-e-x, some parents have started ringing up the school saying that they think it's a disgusting idea.

Leon wasn't at Tae Kwan Do training either Tuesday or Thursday. Selwyn asked after him without making a big deal of it.

We blue belts and red belts spent both training nights going over everything we'd need for the coming Saturday's grading with Master Kim. They were light sessions; I've heard of some instructors who go around whacking people at final training nights with a wooden sword to psych them up. Sounds a bit radical to me — you don't need that if you've worked properly. Anyway, you can get stale if you overtrain too close to a tournament. Other nights during the week, I concentrated on speed work with patterns, and on my patent clothesline-kicker.

There's another grading coming up, too — for white belts and yellow belts — a fortnight after ours, just as the school holidays start. So Selwyn's been working with them as well. If Stacey goes half as well as she's been going at training, she'll be fantastic.

She and her mum and Ham and I walked part of the way home together after both practices. The way Mrs James's face lights up when she looks at Stacey is really touching.

Mum invited them both in for coffee on Thursday night. It had taken a couple of visits before Mrs James relaxed with Mum and Les, but now everyone was at ease and friendly. I wondered if this was what it would be like to have a sister around the place . . . but no, I certainly don't think of Stacey as a sister!

On Saturday morning, nearly the whole club was at the hall by ten o'clock. Even the junior belts who weren't grading had come along to support us. The only ones missing were Trish, who was working, and Leon.

Selwyn took us through a stretch and warm-up routine that lasted twenty minutes. I was starting to wonder if I'd run out of steam before the grading even started. Then we did leg massage on ourselves to keep our muscles relaxed. At exactly ten-thirty the hall door opened and Master Kim walked in.

Master Kim is a springy little Korean guy. He must be over fifty, but he walks and moves like someone half that age. When he sits down he doesn't even rest his back against the chair. He puts his feet squarely on the ground in front of him and sits up absolutely straight. I've seen him stay like that for quarter of an hour without moving a muscle. That's self-discipline for you.

We all stood and bowed to Master Kim, who bowed back. Then he bounced over to Selwyn and gave him a bear hug. It made everyone grin, especially since Selwyn was wearing his gi and Master Kim was in a suit. He always wears a suit when he grades people.

Selwyn called those of us who were grading out onto the floor. I took three deep breaths through my nose, tensed all my muscles, relaxed all my muscles, and let my mind go free. We were under way.

The grading took about forty minutes. Or so

Stacey told me afterwards. It could have been a hundred and forty minutes or four minutes for all I knew. I wasn't aware of time. I was between Josh and Janelle, and whenever I turned to face either of them their eyes stared right through me. I guess mine were the same.

We went through all our patterns. You could hear the slap of bare feet on the floor with each move, and the exploding yells of "Tae Kwan!"

We performed our whole range of kicks and punches against a big pad that Selwyn was holding. I went for controlled power. As I've said before, I'm quite fast, but it's strength I need to work on. Selwyn kept giving me tiny nods of encouragement as my fists and feet smacked into the pad, and that made me go even harder.

Finally, we put on our body-padding and headgear and knocked each other around the floor in pairs. I sparred with Josh, as I knew I was going to. He didn't show me any mercy — I wouldn't have wanted him to — and I used every bit of speed I could. I got thumped a few times, especially with the spinning kicks that Josh is so good at, but I blocked and dodged a few of them, and I landed a couple of good fast roundhouse kicks myself. When Master Kim called "Stop!", he gave us both a quick smile and I felt as if I'd just won Lotto.

We sat down on the floor with the others. I was next to Stacey (instinct, I suppose), and now that it was all over I started to tremble. Stacey grabbed one of my hands with both of hers and squeezed it, which is against every rule of grading behaviour. "That was awesome," she whispered. "Awe-some!"

It would take a week before we got the results from Master Kim. But before he left he came around and shook hands with all of us who'd been grading. He only does that when he's pleased, so we felt pretty pleased too.

Stacey was heading off to do some office cleaning with her mother. "What are you going to do now?" she asked me.

"I'm going to lie in the bath for an hour," I told her. "Then I was going to read a pile of Judge Dredd comics I saw at the gala day, but someone else bought them first."

"You stupid geek!" laughed Stacey. "Why didn't you tell me?" She gave my hand another squeeze and was off.

I had only fifty minutes in the bath. Les and Mum have this strange idea that they should be allowed into the bathroom occasionally, and they were going out after lunch to see one of Les's mates. So I dressed and started creaking around the house, looking for something to read.

The phone rang as Mum and Les were on their way out the door. Mum picked it up. "Oh, hello, Stacey. Do you want to – oh, right . . . right . . . yes, he will . . . what? Those horrible things! . . . Yes, he does . . . No, that'll be fine . . . Yes, sure . . . Bye, Stacey."

"Well?" I asked. As soon as I'd heard it was Stacey, I hung around waiting to talk to her. I couldn't believe it when Mum hung up.

"None of your business," Mum said. "Just girl talk." It was Les's turn to roll his eyes at me this time as he ushered her out the door.

I flicked through all the magazines in the house and found nothing interesting. I checked the TV programmes and found the same. I picked the phone up off its usual place on the floor and gasped because bending over hurt the places where Josh had connected. I phoned a couple of mates and they were both out. I sat around with that flat feeling you get when something you've been looking forward to has been and gone.

I'd just decided I might as well watch a prehistoric movie in black-and-grey when there was a knock on the front door. I hauled myself carefully to my feet, walked gingerly over to the door, and opened it with care.

A pile of Judge Dredd comics was staring me in the face. "Someone said these would help him relax," said a voice from behind the pile.

"Great! Great!" I babbled. "Come in! Come in!" Stop saying everything twice! the voice in my head warned.

I took the comics from Stacey and put them on the living room table. Then I stood back and grinned at her. She was wearing a long denim skirt and the same big white jumper that she'd worn at Josh's party.

I've made it a rule during my long career with females not to say anything about what they wear. I made the rule after one time in the fourth form when I saw a girl I was keen on down town. "Like the dress," I told her, thinking it was quite a cool comment to make. She started giggling and everyone turned around and stared. Turned out the 'dress' was a smock thing she wore for her part-time job at a takeaway bar.

"You should have told me you liked Judge Dredd," she said, pushing her hair back behind her ears. "We could have gone fifty-fifty. Have you got any more of—" She didn't finish the sentence because I kissed her.

I kissed her quite a few more times during the next half hour. I'd never spent time with a girl before who kept kissing me back, so I wasn't going to waste a minute of it.

She kept smiling at me — even when I accidentally bumped her forehead with mine, and even when I went "aaarghh!" because she pressed one of the sore spots where Josh had got me at grading. And she laughed out loud when we were sitting side by side on the sofa and we couldn't work out how to turn and face each other easily. It was a nice laugh though, and I didn't feel embarrassed. A guy can feel stupid if things go wrong.

And, quite suddenly, things did go wrong. I had one arm around Stacey's shoulders — I'd had it there so long it was starting to go to sleep, but hell, I didn't mind if it started to snore! Stacey had her legs tucked up beside her, and she was leaning so that her cheek was against mine.

I was thinking to myself how funny the whole idea of kissing is. I mean, why press your mouths together? Why not your cheeks? Or your noses, or your ears? Or . . . I'd better not go any further with that idea. Kissing might be funny, but it's also quite a pleasant way of passing the time, and I was ready to try again. Stacey certainly didn't seem to mind. She lifted her face up towards mine.

I put my other hand — my not-around-the-shoulders hand — on her hip, just at the top of her thigh. I put it there to balance. No kidding; I was going to fall over against the back of the sofa otherwise. I had my fingers spread, and I could feel her hip bone and where the top of her thigh started to curve towards her bottom.

Stacey went rigid. Not just her leg — her body and her shoulders and even her face were absolutely still. It felt as though she'd suddenly been paralysed.

I got such a shock that I sat up straight and stared at her. Her pupils had gone big and she was breathing in little gasps.

"Hey, what's wrong?" I asked. Then my Tae Kwan Do training took over. "Take deep breaths," I said (which must have sounded a fraction weird). "Start from the stomach. Breathe in slowly."

She tried, and managed a scared sort of smile. But the skin under her eyes and around her nose was pinched and white, and she was shaking. "I'd better go, Chris."

"What's the matter?" I repeated. And — stupidly — "I'm sorry."

"It's okay." Like hell it was. She wouldn't even look at me. "I'd better go."

"Do you want some coffee? How about I walk home with you?"

"No. No — please, Chris. I'd better go." A quarter-smile out of a scared face, and she left.

I sat on the sofa, stared uselessly at the pile of Judge Dredd comics Stacey had brought for me, and tried to understand what had gone wrong. I might have done okay in grading this morning, I was thinking, but I reckon I failed a more important test this afternoon.

Chapter 15

I wondered for a while if I should tell Mum about Stacey. Then I thought, nah — why tell her something she doesn't need to know?

I rang Stacey, though. Both eyes, eh. I'd thought and thought about it, and there was no way I could just ignore what had happened. I wondered if maybe McAndrew had put the hard word on her sometime and upset her. I wouldn't have thought so, though; the guy's not a total animal.

I decided to ask Les a few questions after they came home — really casual, like. I caught up with him in the garage looking at his car. People had kept on turning to stare at it while he was driving back and he was wondering if something was wrong. Wrong! I could have given him a three-page list!

"Les, do you know if Stacey ever had a stepfather, or anything like that?" It wasn't the prettiest way of putting it, but there's one thing I've realised about

Les — he doesn't take offence easily.

"There was one guy for a while," Les said, "but something went wrong. I think . . . I dunno, Karen said she and Stacey had to get away." He leaned against a mudguard, and something inside the car went *graaa-aunch*. "Mind you, I'm not sure if you can believe everything Karen says."

"Why not?"

"Well, she even reckons you're a nice kid!"

I could belt Les sometimes. Half the time you can't tell whether he's kidding or being serious. And it's so irritating when it's something that matters to you.

Les must have seen I was annoyed, because he gave me an it's-the-truth nod. I told him I was going to buckle his car roof by breathing on it. Then I went inside and rang Stacey.

Mrs James answered. She asked me about the grading and I told her I was so battered I could hardly turn the pages of the comics Stacey lent me. I could hear her telling Stacey and laughing.

Stacey's voice, when she came to the phone, was uncertain. "Hi, Chris."

"I've got to make this call as short as I can," I said. "I'm too exhausted to hold the phone for long." I heard her give a shaky sort of laugh. If I could have reached down the phone and hugged her, I would have. "Thanks for the Judge Dredd comics," I told her. "I judge you've got good taste, and I dread giving them back." Stacey made a rude noise at the

132

other end. "But I am bringing them back. I'll drop them over tomorrow morning if that's okay. And I'll go down on my knees and beg for any others you've got." (Can you tell I'd been practising these lines too?)

Stacey's voice was almost normal when she replied, "I'll hold you to that. Thanks, Chris."

"Any time, Shorty."

"What's this 'Shorty' business, anyway, Chris Atkinson?"

"Well, you told me I was quite tall. Do you remember when?"

I got the giggle I was after, said goodbye and hung up. Out in the kitchen Mum started clattering things around to prove she hadn't been listening.

I walked around to Stacey's place late Sunday morning. I hadn't read all the comics but that didn't matter. The guys with the tattoos had bits of an old car spread out on the footpath outside the flats. Maybe I should give Les their address. They said "G'day mate," as I went past staring at the blue and red vulture vanishing down the neck of one guy's shirt.

Ham announced to the whole town that I was ringing his front doorbell, and when Mrs James opened the door he gave me a friendly head butt on the thigh. "Come in, Chris," said Mrs James, and I limped after her.

"Fancy walking all the way over here and then

having to walk straight back," she said. I looked confused. Was this her way of telling me I wasn't welcome?

"Your mum just rang up and invited us over for lunch," Mrs James continued. "I'm getting some doughnuts from the Hot Bread Shop, so —" She seemed to be thinking for a second. " — so I'll go on ahead. Stacey says she'll be ready in a minute if you'd like to wait."

"In two minutes," said a voice from somewhere in the flat. "There's some more Judge Dredds on the table."

I read three comics in the nine minutes it took till Stacey appeared. Her hair was all braided up on top of her head. "Found any big words you can't understand?" she asked, looking a bit shy.

As she locked the door of their flat, Stacey said, "I need this walk. I need to lose some weight."

I gave her a sideways, head-to-toe survey. "Liar," I replied.

We started off down the drive, with Ham bounding around us, behind us and ahead of us all at once. "Okay if I hold your hand?" I asked. "I get lost easily."

Stacey pretended to inspect my fingernails. Just as well I always keep them cut for Tae Kwan Do. "Oh - - okay," she said.

The guys from the end flat looked up as we walked past. "Hey, lady!" one of them with a screaming gorilla on his left arm called. "You don't want a guy who walks you places. We can drive you — soon as we put the car back together!"

Stacey laughed. "I think your car's getting rusty," she said and pointed to where Ham was lifting his leg against one of the engine bits on the footpath.

I cornered Leon in the corridor at school on Tuesday. "Coming to practice tonight?" I asked, as casually as I could.

"Any of your business?" he asked, all macho.

"Yeah, it is, actually. We're in the same club. We help each other, right?"

Leon looked at the wall beside me. "I'm thinking about it."

He didn't come. Neither had the results of our grading. "Nothing yet," announced Selwyn when he arrived. We weren't expecting any news till Thursday at the earliest, but we groaned and booed anyway.

Since the junior belts were doing their grading in a week and a half, we experts spent most of Tuesday evening instructing them. Guess who I got to work with? Or should I say — guess who I made sure I got to work with? And guess who's one of the fastest learners I've ever instructed?

"You ever get worried you'll wear out your bottom lip?" I asked her at the end of training when Selwyn wasn't looking. Stacey looked puzzled so I explained. She wasn't even aware that she did it.

"You're lucky I don't do it when you kiss me," she said. "Then you'd be sorry!"

Wednesday, in PE, Mrs Jennings gave us a Free Activity Lesson, where you can try whatever you like, so long as you're actually doing something active, and not setting fire to the walls. That's always a possibility with some of the guys at our school.

I was vaguely trying to decide between some weight-training and volleyball with a few of the other guys, when Stacey came up to me. With her trackpants she was wearing a T-shirt I hadn't seen before. It read: A WOMAN'S PLACE IS IN THE HOUSE — OF PARLIAMENT.

"Would you be able to take me through my grading patterns again, Chris?" she asked.

We went off to a corner of the gym together, collecting a couple of knowing looks from Stacey's friends as we went. "Right," I said. "Everything from the basic stance, okay?" Stacey nodded.

As always when I'm instructing, I forgot where we were. When I held Stacey's wrist to change the position of her blocking hand, or when I pushed her hip to get her back leg braced more firmly, I never thought that if I was doing these things in any other way, my stomach would be tight. And when I got her to attack me in the whole pattern, kicking and punching, with that final yell of "Tae Kwan!" I never thought what it must look like to anyone watching.

And people were watching. The whole class was watching, as we both realised from the clapping and the "Way to go, Stacey!" as she finished. I felt embarrassed, then pleased for her.

Then a voice came from the back: "Hey, Atkinson can actually fight a girl!" I recognised Dwayne Thatcher's sneer straightaway.

Then McAndrew joined in. "He'd probably fall over if a guy breathed on him!" There were a couple of sniggers from others in the class.

If it had just been about me, I'd have ignored them. That's what Selwyn says to do; that's self-discipline. But I wasn't letting them lay any crap on Stacey. My shoulders stiffened with anger. "Let's find out," I said. "Come on."

The sniggers stopped and things went quiet. "Come on," I said again. Kids turned and looked at Thatcher and McAndrew. They looked at each other. "Come on," I said a third time. "Come and breathe on me."

McAndrew began to move forward. Thatcher didn't. That's pretty much what I'd expected. "Want to start with the basic pattern, then?" I asked McAndrew, perfectly friendly. He blinked in surprise, and I sensed Stacey relax.

Mrs Jennings sang out from the other end of the gym: "Come on, people! Doing, not watching! I want people here for volleyball. Kevin McAndrew and Kelly Hohepa — come and pick teams."

The other kids grumbled, but they went. So did McAndrew, after giving me a look that was mainly puzzled. And so did Thatcher, after giving me a look that was mainly vicious.

When Selwyn came into the hall for Thursday night's grading, six pairs of eyes started burning holes in him. He grinned. "Waiting?" he asked.

We bowed and lined up. Selwyn took a sheet of notepaper out of his pocket. He unfolded it deliberately slowly. He folded it up again and said, "Nice evening, isn't it?" We groaned and moaned, so he unfolded the paper a second time, and began reading Master Kim's grading decisions.

Janelle was now a blue belt. Colin the truck driver was a blue belt red tab. Josh was — Selwyn smiled and we started cheering before he even read it — black belt. Black Belt 1st Dan, which is the lowest, but a black belt nevertheless.

"Chris Atkinson —" Selwyn read. I looked straight ahead. "Second Kup."

Second Kup. I was a red belt. I swallowed. The others cheered. "Congratulations, all," said Selwyn. We all shook hands and banged one another on the back, while Brenda and Wiri and the other junior belts came up and squeaked around us.

Except for Stacey. In front of the whole club, she kissed me on the cheek.

"Whooo-oooo!" went the little kids and the not-so-little kids. My belt wasn't the only thing about me that was now red.

Chapter 16

Last week of term. Funny how it seems the holidays will never come, then suddenly the days at school start shrinking like water going down a plughole, and it's all over before you realise it.

They've postponed those sex education (Human Relationships, sorry) classes for fifth formers. They're thinking of making them voluntary — you can either go or do study. That's just bumming out; everyone's going to choose study, because they want the free time and because they don't want other kids giving them heaps for going to sex lessons.

Pity they didn't postpone holiday assignments, too. I had to do Population Patterns for Geography, Magazine Analysis for English, and the 1930's Depression for History. It gave me a depression of my own just thinking about it.

I also told myself that I was really going to work on my sparring skills. There was just a month-and-a-half till the tournament, and I was determined not to make a fool of myself like I did against that Rick guy last time.

Leon was still keeping his distance from Tae Kwan Do. McAndrew and Thatcher were still keeping their distance from me. I was keeping my distance from Stacey a little bit, too. It isn't easy when you're thinking about someone so much, but I kept remembering her getting so uptight at our place that afternoon.

I didn't see her the weekend just gone. Mum couldn't resist dropping a few hints about my asking her round — light hints, like boulders rolling down a hill.

I expected Les to drop hints as well — his would be like whole avalanches rolling down a hill. But his mind was on other things. First he found a piece of rubber hose lying on the garage floor and couldn't work out where it belonged on the car. Then, when he was kneeling on the concrete looking under the chassis, Mum sneaked up behind and pinched him on the bum. Next thing you know, they're giggling and wrestling in a corner of the garage like a couple of teenagers. Disgusting.

I knew I wouldn't be seeing much of Stacey over the holidays, either. She and her mother were going to stay with some of Mrs James' friends. Les thinks Mrs James might still be looking for geriatric nursing jobs. I know you have to take work where you can get it these days, and I know it sounds selfish, but I hope she doesn't get a job where she and Stacey have to move somewhere else. Not for a while yet.

Training was good on both Tuesday and Thursday. I wore my red belt (ta-ra!). I bought it second-hand from Josh, after he'd taken off the tabs of black insulating tape. I've told Frances she can have my blue belt when she does her next grading, after the baby's born.

We senior belts spent most of the time working with the white belts and yellow belts for Saturday's grading. I didn't try to get Stacey again; that wouldn't be fair to her or to the other kids. I worked with Wiri; it's interesting to instruct someone who has all those extra non-stop arms. And I worked with Brenda; it's even more interesting to instruct someone who's so small you have to bend down to hear what they're asking you.

I walked part of the way home with Stacey and Mrs James both nights, Ham had a sore paw: one of the guys from the other flat accidentally closed his car door on it while Ham was trying to check inside for unwanted dinosaurs. The guys have been bringing him bones and dog biscuits every day since then! Mrs James reckons Ham keeps forgetting which paw to limp on when he sees them coming.

Friday morning: last day of term! Stacey rang.

"I'm a bit nervous about tomorrow's grading," she said. "Could I come round after school and just go through the patterns one last time?"

"No, you can't," I told her. Stacey went silent at the other end, so I gave an evil laugh and went on. "Can I come round to your place instead? Mum's given me this huge great bone for Ham. I think it's meant to be his school holiday present."

"I'll tell him," Stacey said. "Yeah, sure, come round here instead. If you don't mind."

"I haven't got a mind to mind with," I said. I was really in form.

Stacey laughed. "I didn't want to be the one who told you that." Choice: they reckon that if a girl starts insulting you, you can be sure she likes you.

I didn't go straight to Stacey's after school. I had to go home and get Ham's bone first. Since it looked as though it came from the leg of a Tyrannosaurus, I'd decided not to take it to History or English. Anyway, that meant I could have a shower and change out of my glamorous school uniform.

When Stacey opened the flat's door, Ham started leaping and bounding all around me. When I opened the plastic bag with his bone in, he started pretending to limp on all four paws at once. I told Stacey my great discovery. "That Ham is a ham!"

She was standing near me, like she had the first time I kissed her. But I just said, "Do you want to go though your patterns, then?"

Stacey looked a bit disappointed. "All right," she said. "Would you like a cup of coffee first?"

"She's right, thanks. Let's talk about what you're supposed to know for tomorrow."

"All right," Stacey said again in a flat sort of voice. She sat down on one end of the sofa. I hesitated and then sat down in a chair opposite. She looked at me for a second, then looked away.

We talked through all the things she needed to know for the next day's grading. I couldn't see why Stacey was feeling nervous; she knew everything — name, order, every detail. She didn't seem very pleased about it, though; her answers sounded almost angry and she just stared at the carpet.

Ham was grinding at his bone outside the living-room window. We could hear him in the silence after Stacey had answered my last question. She looked up and smiled at me.

"Ham likes his present," she said.

"Let's go through your defensive patterns once more," I told her. It must have sounded pretty rude, I suppose. Stacey obviously thought so.

Her smile vanished. "Only if you've got the time," she said.

"Sorry?" I suddenly felt stupid.

"Well, you seem to be in a big rush or something. I don't want to hold you up if you're busy." Her cheeks were pink by now.

"It's okay," I said, still feeling stupid.

"Like hell!" At the sound of Stacey's raised voice through the window, Ham stopped grinding and started growling. "Ever since you got here you've been so—so unfriendly. Are you in a hurry to go?"

"Look, I just don't want—" I was sounding more

of a dork by the second. "I just don't want to put pressure on you or anything."

Stacey shot up from the sofa. She was angry, the way she had been after the school disco, and that time at school when I'd ignored her during Tae Kwan Do. She even stamped her foot. "Don't be so stupid! How can you put pressure on me?"

I stood up, too. We must have looked like something out of a TV soap.

"Look, Stacey, you know how you got so upset that time at our place — the afternoon after my grading?" Stacey stared away. I stumbled on. "Well, I don't— I'm not gonna make you feel like that again, right? I'm not going to do anything that hassles you. That's all."

Stacey's bottom lip was trembling. She bit her teeth into it. Then she opened her mouth to say something. Instead she took three strides over to me and put her arms around me.

She said nothing for the next couple of minutes, just kept her arms tight around me while I kept mine around her. Her breath was warming the front of my T-shirt, and other bits of her were warming other bits of me.

Then she said, "Chris Atkinson, you are so thick!"

"Maybe, but I'm handsome with it," I replied.

"That last time" she went on "— at your place. It wasn't your fault."

I waited to see if she was going to say any more, but she didn't; just kept warming my T-shirt for a while. Then she stepped away and gave me a quick reverse punch on the ribs.

"Come on, red belt," she said. "Let's do this pattern."

I was wrong about Stacey's grading the next morning. I thought she'd be good, but she wasn't. She was great.

The others did well, too. Master Kim always enjoys grading the junior belts, because the little ones are so bouncy and eager. He grinned at Brenda, especially when Selwyn had to kneel down on the ground and hold the pad for her to kick; she's not tall enough to reach it if he holds it up in the air the usual way. He grinned at Wiri as Wiri windmilled away with his patterns.

But he nodded when he was watching Stacey. She just flowed through things, yet you could feel the concentration in her. After she finished, everyone clapped. Stacey went pink, which made a nice combination with her white gi.

Stacey went away for most of the next two weeks with her Mum. I planned to train flat out, to do something resembling work on my History and Geography and English assignments, and maybe help Les with a bit of plastic surgery on his car.

Oh, and I had a few mornings' lawn-mowing and hedge-trimming lined up at the Polytech. Laidback Les, who seems to have made friends with everyone there, jacked it up. I was a bit slacked off at first, him deciding to organise my holiday for me, but the money will come in handy. Any money will come in handy!

It would all help to keep me busy, and stop me thinking about Stacey all the time.

Who was I kidding! I'd even started having dreams about her. No, I'm not going to tell you what happens in the dreams: I'm thinking of selling the script rights to one of those Adults-Only film companies.

Chapter 17

Believe it or not, I did some of the things I planned to do in the holidays.

I worked on my school assignments. I turned over a couple of new leaves for the Magazine Analysis one. I got Population Patterns all figured out. I brightened up the Depression. I'm actually finishing most assignments and handing them in these days! My teachers may need to see Mrs Jennings for some counselling.

I worked on the Polytech's lawns a few mornings, and got paid some useful gold. Hey, there are some choice girls going to Polytech! I could start re-thinking my future career.

Poor old Les ("poor old Les!") might have to do some career rethinking too. Or just plain career thinking. Mum got stuck into him about how he was okay at finding jobs for other people, but he didn't seem interested in finding one for himself.

Les tried to laugh it off. "It's all right—" he started saying, like he did every other time.

"Les, it's not all right!" Mum snapped. "I'm tired of being the only person in this house who worries about where the next dollar's coming from!"

She stamped out of the living room. Les looked at me, grinned and shook his head. But she must have got through to him, because he didn't even make a sick joke.

Since Les had got me the Polytech job, I bought him a present with some of my earnings. A car horn that makes the sound of a bull elephant trumpeting when you press it. Other drivers already keep well away from Les's Rustmobile, and the horn should give him even more clear space at intersections.

I worked hard on my build-up towards tournament, too. I did a lot of practice on blocks. A light guy like me (all right — a skinny guy like me) has to avoid getting hit if possible, so I concentrated on knife-blocks using the edge of my hand, and X-blocks with both hands held low together in front. I went for a few runs and pushed myself for stamina. I met Dwayne Thatcher smoking one night, and we ignored each other. I met Kevin McAndrew running in the opposite direction the next night (rugby training, I suppose), and we grunted at each other.

We took it easy on club nights. A lot of kids were away on holiday. Even Selwyn was away one night; you tend to forget he's got a home and a family and a builder's job outside Tae Kwan Do. Josh wasn't there

148

either, so red belt Chris Atkinson ran a Thursday practice.

We did some self-defence work, talking about things you can use against an attacker — jabbing a book under their nose, stabbing them with car keys, ramming the spike of an umbrella in places I'd rather not mention. Janelle reckons I'd better be careful at the next school disco.

She also wondered out loud why I'd come to practice, since a certain white belt wasn't there. I made her do thirty press-ups for being cheeky to the senior belt, but I didn't mind. It's okay being kidded, even by third-formers. Makes you feel important.

Anyhow, the time passed quite quickly. I got a card from Stacey with a brief message reading "Shorty says keep fit." Les announced he was going to test the card for invisible ink to see what else she'd written.

I was going to say something smart, but stopped myself. Mum and he had made up after their Get-a-job-Les argument, and I didn't want to throw a spanner in the lovey-dovey works.

I spent a lot of time thinking about Stacey, before and after the card. It makes for some great fantasies! But you don't need to be a psychiatrist to realise that something pretty frightening happened to her when she was younger. I wish she'd tell me about it, but that's up to her.

I was lying on the sofa a few days later, reading some Judge Dredds I'd bought with my Polytech mowing money, when the phone went. Mum got to it before I could, and I knew straightaway it was Stacey. (That's because Mum said, "Oh hello, Stacey.") She and Mum chatted away for a totally unnecessary length of time, but finally I got my turn.

"Yes?" I asked. "Who is this speaking, please?"

"It's the voice of your conscience," Stacey replied. "And I bet you can't spell 'conscience'. Hey," she went on, "is there any news about my belt?"

The grading results for Stacey and the others wouldn't be announced till the next Thursday. Selwyn was waiting for everyone to get back from holiday.

"I can give you a belt now if you like," I told her. "How about a belt on the backside?" I suddenly thought of what she'd told me about the scar she had there, and the voice inside my head started making colourful suggestions.

"How's Ham?" I asked quickly.

"Fat!" Stacey said. "Typical Ham — he kept telling the guy who runs the kennels that he was starving, and now he's come back looking like a stuffed Ham. I'm just going to take him for a walk. You doing anything?"

Yes, I was doing something. Quarter of an hour later I was helping Stacey take Ham for a walk.

I'd even ridden around to her place on my bike, super-uncool though it is. One of the guys with tats (snakes and tigers' heads on both hands — maybe he works for the RSPCA) was wandering down the drive as I pedalled and squeaked up it. "Hey, man! How many cc's?" he said.

I talked to Mrs James for a few minutes. Turns out she didn't make any job applications after all, so I needn't have worried about that. "I like living in this town," she said. "It's a good place."

Stacey had more to say about it soon after she and I set off along the footpath. Ham was waddling ahead, looking hopefully for friendly kennel owners.

"Mum feels she can make a fresh start here," she said. "She's got friends, like Les and your mum. She's got the cleaning job at Polytech. She says we can both pick up things again here."

I nodded. I could guess what Mrs James meant. I'd seen it happen with Mum and Laughing Les. I hoped it happened for her and Stacey.

We strolled on around a few more corners. Stacey was telling me about a boy cousin of hers she'd been keen on when she was about thirteen. "Now he wears all this weird punk gear — and his Mum has to steal his jeans to put them in the wash. He's gross!"

Maybe so, but I still felt jealous of him. I was feeling kind of shy, too, after not seeing Stacey for nearly two weeks, and I think she might have felt the same. But then her hand slipped into mine — or was it the other way around? — and we walked on like that. Ham looked at us, snorted, and started investigating the trees at the park we'd just reached.

"I had a dream about you," Stacey said suddenly.

My ears pricked up. "Yeah? What happened?"

151

There was silence, and I asked again. "What happened?" When I turned towards Stacey, she was looking at the ground and the back of her neck was pink. "It's too embarrassing to describe," she said.

I pretended to be shocked. "You wicked woman!" I said. "I'll tell my mother!"

We were in among the trees, and we stopped. Stacey turned to face me and I kissed her. I did it really smoothly — or so I thought. Then she said, "Your heart's thumping away like a train."

"Well, I have been doing a lot of *train*ing," I replied.

"Sick joke!" Stacey protested. Then without any warning, she screamed and jumped. I yelled and jumped. Ham barked and jumped.

Ham barked because I yelled. I yelled because Stacey screamed. And Stacey screamed because Ham had come silently up behind me and pushed his big wet nose against her hand where she had it round my waist.

We walked on across the park. "Typical!" I said to Stacey. "Absolutely typical! I bet I'm the only guy in the whole country who makes a girl scream when he kisses her."

At Thursday practice in the final week of the holidays, everyone was back, except for Leon — and Frances, of course. Selwyn called us to order, we bowed, and he produced Master Kim's list for the white and yellow belts.

I crossed my fingers for Stacey.

Wiri was a white belt with yellow tabs. So was little Brenda, who started jumping up and down on the spot till Selwyn gave her a look. Tae Kwan Do teaches that you should keep calm and modest when you win something.

The other belts had all done well, too. Everyone had passed their grading. Everyone except the name I was listening for. There was no mention of Stacey.

I couldn't believe it. I'd seen how well she'd done. I'd seen Master Kim nod with approval. Yet her name wasn't on the list. There had to be a mistake.

"Congratulations, all you successful graders," said Selwyn, starting to fold up the paper. Silence spread as other people realised Stacey's name was missing. I was in the front row so I couldn't turn and look at her. I wouldn't have dared, anyway.

Then Selwyn started to smile. "Oh, I nearly forgot . . . Congratulations to another person too. Stacey James — 8th Kup."

8th Kup! Stacey had gone straight from white to yellow belt, missing out the halfway yellow tabs. She'd double-graded! It hardly ever happens with Master Kim. It had never happened to me. But she'd done it!

Cheering and clapping started up all round the hall. Selwyn clapped as well.

I turned round to look at Stacey. She was blushing and grinning from earlobe to earlobe. She grabbed little Brenda, who was standing next to her, and gave her a hug. "Congratulations, Brenda," she said.

"Congratulations, Stacey," a voice squealed back. There were more cheers and clapping.

I felt as pleased as if I'd double-graded myself. Just think how well Stacey might do at tournament. Just think how neat it would be if the whole term were to go as well as this!

Chapter 18

You should have seen Mrs James when she heard about Stacey. I was dying to tell her the moment we got outside, but I managed to restrain myself and let her daughter tell her. Mrs James' face opened up in that smile that makes her look more like Stacey's elder sister, and she gave the new yellow belt a hug. Ham nudged my leg in a pleased sort of way; I hope to get off with light bruising.

Stacey was doing so well that Selwyn was thinking of letting her go in for the tournament — the tournament that was just over a month away, as I hardly needed to remind myself.

Some clubs enter all their members in tournaments, even the youngest white and yellow belts, but Selwyn's not keen on that. In tournaments you're grouped by size as much as by belt, so you could end up fighting someone who's much more experienced than you, and get really wasted.

But Selwyn reckoned Stacey could enter if she wanted to. She had a couple of weeks to decide and in the meantime she was going to do some extra training. "It'll help me lose weight," she said.

It's incredible. I heard Janelle speaking to her mates at practice last week, wishing she could put on more weight. True, she's all bones and elbows like a lot of girls her age, but she looks perfectly okay. And Stacey looks more than okay! Why do girls worry when they don't need to?

By the time we'd been back at school for a couple of days, it felt as if we'd never been away – as usual.

Mrs Jennings was wearing a new maroon tracksuit with gold stripes, and a maroon headband. Very charming. Thatcher and McAndrew were wearing the same old dirty looks, and Leon was still pathetically hanging around after them — which was especially pathetic considering the way they treat him.

I saw them Tuesday lunchtime, on my way to practise some blocks in the school gym.

Thatcher and McAndrew had Leon down on his back, on the grass beside the rugby field. McAndrew was kneeling on Leon's biceps so he couldn't move, and cuffing the side of Leon's head in a fairly harmless way. But Thatcher was standing on the palms of Leon's hands one after the other, grinding his heels in. You could tell it was hurting; Leon couldn't stop a couple of half-yells coming out.

I don't know if Thatcher had seen me or not, but

he started jeering at Leon. "Come on, pink belt! Are your handy-pandys getting sorey-worey?"

I thought for a second about getting involved. I decided Leon wouldn't thank me, so I kept going towards the gym. Thatcher got louder. "Tae Kwan Do! Shit, you lot couldn't even tie your shoelaces!"

All afternoon I kept telling myself: you should have; you shouldn't have; you should have; you shouldn't have.

The other planet-shaking news from the first couple of days back was that, first, the sex education (yeah, let's call them that) lessons were going to happen after all, and would be for everyone in the fifth form . . . shock, horror, gasp!

And second, my holiday assignments all came back with comments starting "You should have . . ." which says everything you need to know about my holiday assignments.

But there was one ray of sunshine at school. Stacey and I were to do an English assignment together, on a novel called *1984*. Even though the title's about ten years out of date, it's still a pretty good and disturbing story.

So of course, since we were doing the project together, we had to get together, didn't we? I asked Mum if it would be all right for Stacey to come round to our place one afternoon and work with me.

"Certainly, love. You've been teaching her how to kick; maybe she can teach you how to spell." I looked dignified, and ignored her and Les. I think it's

157

pathetic when grown-ups snigger, and I think it's tragic to see Mum picking up these evil habits from Les.

Stacey came around on Friday afternoon. She arrived at the same time Mum got home, so it was all very respectable. We even did some work on *1984*. Mum was right; Stacey can spell better than me. Mind you, you don't have to be very brilliant to do that.

Mum and Les were going down to the pub for an hour or so with some of Les's mates. They often do on Fridays. Mum says she's turned into a really heavy drinker since she met Les; now she can drink a whole shandy in an hour, instead of half a one.

While we were waiting for Layabout Les to get home from Polytech, I made coffee and fruitcake for Mum and Stacey and me. Well, I made the coffee, and lifted the fruitcake out of its supermarket wrapper.

Meanwhile, I eavesdropped on the two females in the living room. "Your Mum must be proud of the way you're getting on at Tae Kwan Do," my mum was saying.

"Yeah, she is, I suppose," I heard Stacey say. There was a pause, and then she added, "Too proud, almost."

Now who does that remind me of? I thought. But Mum laughed.

"You should hear me when young whatsisname in

the kitchen there does well," she said. "I paint it on the sides of the buildings! All parents are the same."

Young whatsisname stood in the kitchen with his mouth hanging open for a few seconds, thinking how mums can sometimes surprise you with their common sense. Then whatsisname came through with three lots of coffee and fruitcake, looking modest. Les came in the front door, so whatsisname had to go back for a fourth cup, looking bad-tempered.

We sat and talked for half an hour or so. Stacey gets along so well with Mum. She still seems a bit uncertain with Les — mind you, his sense of humour would make anyone uncertain, especially about whether to keep living.

But I suspect Les may have noticed more than I'd realised. He went to put his arm around Stacey's shoulders at one stage when he was teasing her, but stopped himself before anyone except me noticed. He's in an extra good mood just now; extra good even for Les.

In fact, he and Mum were so relaxed and chatty that I began to think they'd never make it to the pub. But finally Les looked at his watch and said to Mum, "Come on then, love. All your rough mates in the lounge bar will be missing you."

"I'd better be going too," said Stacey, politely but not very enthusiastically.

"Hang on," I told her. "You haven't finished explaining *1984* to me yet."

"Bully!" she said, and started carrying cups out to the kitchen.

I saw Mum and Les safely out the front door, counted twenty while I waited to see if either of them had forgotten anything, then went back into the living room.

Stacey was standing in the middle of the floor, pushing her hair back behind her ears. "Okay," she said, all brisk and efficient, "what do you want to do with *1984*?"

"I'd sooner do something with this year," I said. Recognise a pre-planned line when you hear one? "This year, this day, this time, this place."

"Smart arse," said Stacey, and poked her tongue out at me. It's a disgusting habit, so it served her right that I kissed her on it just half a second later.

"Aw, yukk!" she went, and wiped her mouth.

"All right! All right!" I said. "So I don't know how to kiss properly."

"I didn't mean—" she started.

"It's no use!" I said. "I'm terribly hurt and offended. You'd better just show me how it's done."

Stacey looked at me uncertainly for a second, then reached her face up towards mine.

"Oh Stacey!" I said, just as she was about to touch me. "You will be gentle with me, won't you?"

Stacey collapsed against me with a snort. "You slimeball!" she laughed. We stood there with our arms around each other, sniggering in each other's ears like two idiots. Then she looked at me again, turned her face up towards me, and pressed her mouth against mine. It was the most amazing kiss I've ever had, and it came with just a tiny taste of fruitcake.

"How's that?" she asked when she'd finished.

"Aw, not bad," I replied. "You're getting better."

"Getting better!" Stacey said. "I'll show you!" She put her hands around the back of my neck and pulled my head down. She kissed me and kept kissing me. After the first eight seconds, I think my toes started sweating.

"Well?" she said when we came up to breathe.

"Help! Help!" I said. We both started to laugh again. Stacey's face had gone shiny, and another little spot, on her chin this time, had turned pink.

We stood quietly with her head against my shoulder for a while. Everything felt safe and peaceful, except that I was starting to have hair problems. Stacey's hair, not mine. Finally I had to pull away from her.

"What's the matter?" Stacey asked.

"You're getting up my nose, Shorty James. Well, your hair is, anyway."

"I'll buy myself a hairnet," said Stacey. "No — I'll buy you a mask, like doctors wear." She put one hand against my side. "I can count your ribs," she told me, and started doing just that.

"Oh yeah?" I pretended to be insulted — after all, it had got pretty good results a few minutes ago. "So I'm skinny, huh?"

"No you're not." Stacey kept counting and I was starting to feel ticklish. "I like you slim. Guys make a stupid big deal out of being all muscley."

Maybe she was thinking of Kevin McAndrew. Whatever, it was reassuring to hear her say she liked non-Mr Universe types.

"Anyway," Stacey went on. "It's better than needing to lose weight like I do."

"You don't!" I told her. "Bet I can count your ribs too." I put my hand on her side, just as she'd done to me. And of course my hand ended up half on one of her breasts.

Stacey gave a little gasp and tensed up, just like that other time when I'd put my hand on her hip. I felt wild with myself because I'd said I wasn't going to frighten her again, and I'd already gone and bloody done it.

Yet even while this thought was tearing through my mind, I was thinking how marvellous she felt against my hand, all soft and curved. Hell, girls are neat!

"No, Chris," Stacey said in my ear. My ears heard her, my brain knew what she meant, but my hand had developed a mind of its own. It stayed where it was.

"No!" Stacey said, loudly this time. She gave me a shove that Selwyn and Master Kim would have admired. It sent me backwards across the room, and I ended up against a table, with my mouth open and my hand still held out like a traffic cop looking for a rushhour. I must have looked a first-class nerd.

"Sorry," I mumbled. I felt hot and stupid.

Stacey stared at the ground. "It's all right," she said.

Suddenly, I seemed to see a lot of things clearly. "It's not all right!" I said loudly. So loudly that Stacey glanced up at me. "Look — you're allowed to say no. I'll bend over and you can kick me."

"I thought you'd get angry," Stacey said. "Think I was just being a tease and getting you worked up."

"That's crap," I said. "You're not like that at all."

Stacey looked at the floor again. "I like you," she said, "and I like kissing you."

"So you should," I said, modestly. "I'm fantastic."

"But if anyone touches me like — like then — I get scared. It was what — when —" She stopped and started to shake.

"Hey, come on," I said. "Come on." I moved across and put my arms around her tightly. She stayed there, shivering against me. If I had to choose anyone to shiver against me, it would be Stacey James.

After a while, she spoke in a voice muffled against my neck. "You're neat, Chris." A big silly grin started rearranging my face.

"There's just one thing I'd like to know," I told Stacey. I felt her tense up again, though not as much as last time. I went on. "I'd like to know why they give us such difficult books as *1984* for English assignments."

Chapter 19

I walked Stacey home a bit later. We met two of the guys with tats. (One guy has DEATH RULES on one bicep and HELLO MUM on the other.) "G'day, lady," they said to Stacey. "Sure you wouldn't prefer us older men?" I got another headbutt on the leg from Ham. Then I came home, had a cold shower, went for a run, came home again, and had a hot shower. Having a girlfriend like Stacey is not good for power-saving and water economy!

There were only two-and-a-bit weeks left till tournament. Two-and-a-bit weeks till revenge! Revenge on myself, mainly. I wanted to prove that I wasn't as much of a fool as I looked last time.

I pushed myself hard at the club and at home, aiming to peak at tournament. I wanted to know all my sparring techniques and moves so well that I could fight with what Selwyn calls an empty mind —

just letting my reflexes take over. I wanted to be physically and mentally tough enough that if I got hurt I could keep going. It's not a macho thing; it's more of a discovery. Really fierce training means you find out things about yourself. Besides, it helped keep my mind off a certain Stacey James.

Stacey trained with me some of the time. Not just at the club; at our place, too. She came round a couple of afternoons and we went through sparring routines together. She'd decided to enter the tournament, which I reckon is a great idea. She should do well.

It's choice, training with her. She works hard. She encourages me, and she makes some really good suggestions. And she certainly stops training from getting boring. Once, when we were practising punches and arm blocks against each other, without making any real contact, she knocked away one of my punches with an excellent outside block. Then she stepped straight forward, put her arms around my chest (it's not difficult, given the narrowness of my chest), and hugged me.

"You can't do that in a tournament!" I squawked.

"Why not?" she said. "Could confuse the opposition."

It certainly confused me. I had to have an extra-long cold shower after yesterday's training.

I felt really good about Stacey by this stage. I just wished I knew how I could help her feel less frightened.

That Friday I asked Mrs Jennings if I could use the school gym at lunchtime to do some more practice on my patterns. The gym's got the same sort of floor as the hall at tournament, and it helps if you're used to the surface.

Stacey didn't want to do lunchtime practices. She probably didn't want any more of Thatcher and McAndrew and their nasty cracks. But she came along to watch me on Friday. Other kids were playing volleyball in the gym, including Leon, who pretended not to see me.

I went through my full pattern twice. I was standing and taking deep breaths before starting again, when this slow hand-clapping began from the seats up against the wall. When the voice came, it was like a rerun of the last time.

"Hey, Atkinson, you any good at fighting someone who's really there?"

I ignored him, and got into my stance for the pattern.

"Going to do a little dance for us, are ya, Atkinson?" Thatcher wasn't about to give up.

Then McAndrew joined in. "Ever get frightened about taking on someone else, Atkinson?"

There were a fair number of sniggers from round the gym now, though none from Leon. Stuff this, I thought. I've had enough. I made my voice as calm as possible. "When you're ready," I said. And then, when neither of them moved. "Come on. Let's find out."

Even this was the same as last time. Thatcher just sat and sneered. McAndrew got up uncertainly, then moved forward.

I stood where I was as he came towards me. He stopped about a metre away, looking a bit unsure. He's a big strong guy, I was thinking. No use trying brute strength against him.

I was in a ready stance, weight on both feet, hands held low in front of me. McAndrew watched me carefully. He had his fists up like a boxer.

I tried one more time. "We don't have to do this, you know."

"Aw, diddums!" Thatcher again. "Thought you'd pike out when it got real."

Okay, I told myself. Let's get it over with. I took a couple of fast steps towards him, and brought my right leg up in the start of a roundhouse kick. Then, as McAndrew turned to stop my foot, I brought the leg back down again, whipped my right arm forward, and slapped him across the nose with the back of my knuckles.

It's a move that's meant to anger your opponent, make them lose their cool. McAndrew lost his, all right. He snapped his head back, swore, and charged straight at me.

I was amazed at how instinctively my training took over. I let him come, then I dropped down sideways on my left hand and knee, swept my right leg in a scythe kick, and knocked his feet from under him. He went down with a thud on his bum.

He was up again like a flash. Speed and guts as well as strength, I realised as he came at me again. He swung a big fist at my head. I partly stopped it with a forearm block, but some of the swing made contact with my shoulder. Ooff! the voice inside my head complained.

McAndrew tried to grab me with his other hand. I went forward inside his arm, jabbed the heel of my hand into his jaw so his teeth rattled, and dodged away to the left.

McAndrew's face must have hurt like hell, but he was still ready to fight. He charged at me with both fists up. I didn't want another clout on the shoulder like the last one, so when he was halfway towards me I jumped, pivoted on my left foot, and hit him with a spinning reverse kick. My foot punched his hands into his chest, winding him. He folded up and staggered backwards, holding his ribs.

There were yells and whistles from the onlookers. I looked around and realised that heaps more kids had poured into the gym to watch the fight. Leon's mouth was wide open. Thatcher was half out of his seat, eyes bulging. Stacey was absolutely still. McAndrew tried to come at me again, but he was looking shaky. I suddenly felt ashamed.

"Look," I started to say, "I don't—"

"All right!" said a voice. "Everybody out of the gym unless they're playing something!" It was Mrs Jennings, looking more businesslike than usual. She headed towards us, shooing the other kids out the door as she did so. "Something the matter, you two?" she asked.

"Nah, it's cool," McAndrew said. I stared at him in surprise.

So did Mrs Jennings. "It doesn't look too cool from here," she said.

"It's okay!" McAndrew said, louder. He turned and pushed past Thatcher towards the door. He must have been feeling pretty sore, but he was trying not to show it. Mrs Jennings looked after him, looked at me, shrugged her shoulders and walked away.

I walked over to Stacey. She stood up, and glared at me. "You really made him look a fool, didn't you?" she said.

"He and Thatcher started it!" I protested.

Stacey brushed this aside. "You didn't have to show him up like that," she said.

"Oh, come on!" I was getting annoyed too, and as I got annoyed I got jealous. "You sound like you're still his girlfriend." The moment the words were out, I could have chewed my tongue off.

Stacey glared at me. "I'm not his girlfriend. He doesn't own me. Nobody owns me!" She whirled around and strode away.

Chapter 20

It was obvious that I hadn't impressed Stacey by
fighting Kevin McAndrew. But I hadn't done it to
impress Stacey anyway. I'd done it because I was
sick of being hassled. Still, I should have realised
that a girl who can't stand the macho, caveman
approach wasn't going to think much of the way I
decked him.

I wasn't very impressed by it myself. Tae Kwan
Do discipline says I should have just kept on
ignoring McAndrew and Thatcher. Selwyn would be
annoyed if he knew.

Friday night I did some clothesline-kicking, and
every time I swung my foot, I felt as if I should be
kicking myself. The trouble was, I couldn't stop
feeling these little flickers of pleasure as well,
remembering how that scythe kick dropped
McAndrew. Tae Kwan Do works!

I rang Stacey on Saturday morning. When the

receiver was picked up, I thought the Jameses must be teaching their old dog new tricks. Ham boomed into the mouthpiece. Then Mrs James spoke. "Hello?. . . Oh, hello, Chris . . . No, he treats the phone the way he does someone knocking on the door — should stop anyone trying to sell us things by telephone . . . Yes, she is . . . Hang on, I'll get her."

I heard Mrs James calling to Stacey, and I heard Stacey answering. Then Mrs James and then Stacey again. I could pick up bits of what Stacey was saying, and it didn't sound promising. ". . . busy . . . tell him . . . at school . . . Monday." Then Mrs James's voice: "Well, at least talk to Chris yourself."

"Sorry," I said when Stacey finally came on the phone, "I've rung at a bad time, eh?"

Her voice was frosty. "No . . . well, it's just that I've got all this Chemistry and Maths to do. I should be getting on with it."

I was startled by my own next words: "I suppose it's Kevin McAndrew?"

"No, it's—" Stacey started. Then she took a breath and said, "Well, yes, it is. Not the way you mean, though. I just hate seeing anyone hurt like that. Especially by you, Chris. You didn't need to, did you?"

I sidestepped the question. "He wasn't all that hurt. He'll just have some bruises."

Stacey sighed, and I could hear the disappointment in her voice. "You know what I mean, Chris. Look, I'd better go. I've got heaps of work, truly."

I should have let her hang up, but I had to hurt myself one more time. "Do you want to do any training this weekend? Tournament's two weeks today, remember?"

Stacey hesitated. "I–I'll ring you if I can, okay?"

That meant no. I felt angry. "Not if it's a bother. See ya." I hung up, feeling flat. And as if that wasn't bad enough, Mum had been in the dining room just long enough to hear some of what I'd been saying. And just long enough to misunderstand.

She started in on me when I went into the kitchen to grab some fruit juice. "Chris, I know it's none of my business, but try not to upset Stacey, won't you? You're important to that girl."

Butt out, Mum, I thought. I don't need you giving me a hard time too. I opened my mouth to tell her she'd got it all wrong, but she lifted her hand to stop me.

"No, I don't mean to be nosy, love. But think about it, eh?"

Maybe she was worried I was going to turn out like my old man — the love-em-and-leave-em type. Hell, I should be so lucky!

Feeling misunderstood by the whole world, I wandered out to the garage.

Les had just struck oil . . . there was a pool of it on the garage floor beneath the car. He was standing with his hands on his hips, looking at it and muttering.

"If you want to do some weight-training, you can

172

pick this car up and throw the muddy thing away,"
he told me. I think he said "muddy".

"In a minute," I said. "Les, do you understand
women?"

Les grinned at me. "I hope not," he said, then
added, "But it helps if you listen."

I thought he meant listen to him, so I stared at him
for a moment, waiting, till I caught on. "I do listen,"
I told him.

"That's good," Les said. "And be ready to step
back a bit, eh?"

Les seems to have got a lot more sensible lately.
Must be the extra time he's been spending at
Polytech. I went for a walk, kicked a few lampposts,
and tried to work out what he meant. Mum and I
could both try stepping back a bit, I suppose.

I worked as hard as I could at training, both
Saturday and Sunday. Les helped me with pad work,
and Mum fussed over him afterwards. I kicked the
clothesline so hard that I ended up with raised red
marks across both feet. I missed Stacey. I thought
about Les's advice, and even on Sunday night, when
I was trying to make sense out of *1984*, I didn't ring
her.

I kept watching for her at school on Monday morning. I saw just about everyone else I knew. First it
was Dwayne Thatcher. "I'm glad I'm not you, boy,"
he sneered as he went past.

"Yeah?" I said. "Well that makes us equal. I'm

173

glad I'm not you, either." He gave me the fingers and kept going. I watched as he went to see if I could see the slime trail behind him.

Next I saw Janelle, who came skipping up with her usual pack of mates. "Hey, guess what's happened?"

"All turd-formers have been abolished?" I suggested hopefully.

"Nah!" she said. "Leon's coming back to Tae Kwan Do! He said he'll be there tomorrow night for practice."

I wondered if it was because of the way I decked McAndrew. It'd be just like Leon to do the right thing for the wrong reason.

Round the next corner I came face to face with Kevin McAndrew.

We both looked at each other. We both looked away from each other and we both kept walking. But I was struck by the expression on his face. He looked awkward and a bit pissed off. But there wasn't any of the sneer and threat I'd got from Thatcher. I was still thinking about this when I turned corner number three or four and met Stacey.

She was walking slowly along the corridor towards me, holding her bag against her jumper with both arms, the way girls do, with her grey uniform skirt and white socks below. She had her head bent, looking at the floor, and I could see the part in her hair.

It was a couple of seconds before she realised someone was in front of her, and looked up. It was just enough time to feel like a peeping tom.

When Stacey saw it was me, she looked embarrassed at first. Then she gave me a smile that kept creeping bigger and bigger.

"Hi. You look like you're on your way to something exciting, like Physics, maybe?" I said.

"Worse," said Stacey, and pulled a face. "It's Maths. And I haven't finished my assignment properly."

Join the club, kid, I thought. And then I realised — hey, so she really did have a Maths assignment over the weekend! I felt better. We looked at each other again.

"I'm sorry ab—" we began at the same time. We both stopped and laughed.

"After you," Stacey said.

"No, ladies first," I said. "After you."

She hesitated a moment, then said, "I'm sorry about the weekend. I didn't mean to be so unfriendly. But I was upset."

I nodded. "Yeah, well I go back further than that. I'm sorry about Friday. I know that's why you were upset."

Stacey's teeth nibbled at her bottom lip. I've kissed that bottom lip, I told myself. "I think you should apologise," she said.

Apologise for having kissed her? Then I got my mind together again. "I just did apologise," I said.

"No, I mean to Kevin McAndrew."

We moved over against the wall to avoid a goggling and giggling gaggle of third formers.

175

Apologise to McAndrew? No way! Absolutely no way. I had to make that clear from the start.

"You reckon?" I mumbled.

"Yes, Chris. He was absolutely — humiliated. You didn't have to make him look a complete fool, did you?" I shrugged, and Stacey went on. "I know it was his fault, too — his and Thatcher's. But Thatcher's just a rat, and anyway, you're much more mature than either of them."

Me? Mature? Suddenly I knew what Les meant when he said he hoped that he'd never understand women. Oh, hell, I thought. Oh, all right.

"Okay," I told her.

"You'll apologise? Oh Chris, that's neat! You're neat!"

"I'll apologise . . . tomorrow," I said.

"Tomorrow! Oh, all right. I'll ring you up tonight, eh? And remember practice tomorrow. See ya — red belt."

She reached out, quite unworried by the third formers all watching from the other end of the corridor, and squeezed my hand. Then she swung off towards Maths, back straight and hair bouncing. I slouched off towards Geography.

Chapter 21

Stacey rang me on Monday night, as she said she would. I rushed in from the garage where I'd been doing bench-presses, and Mum handed me the phone with a pleased smile on her face.

"Am I the sort of girl who makes you come running?" Stacey asked when she heard me puffing.

"No. You're the sort of girl who makes me work up a sweat," I replied, perfectly truthfully.

"Flattery will get you nowhere," said Stacey. "But you can keep trying."

We talked about her Maths assignment, and Ham, and Leon coming back to Tae Kwan Do (Stacey's pleased about that), and tomorrow's first Sex Education discussion. ("Let's compare notes afterwards," she said, which made my stomach do a handstand.)

Then she asked, "Are you going to talk to Kevin tomorrow?"

I wish she wouldn't call him Kevin. It sounds too friendly. I said, "Yeah. I will."

"Just tell him you got carried away. Say you didn't mean to make him look a fool in front of everyone."

"All right, Grandma," I said. Stacey blew a raspberry at the other end of the phone.

Actually, I'd already worked out what I was going to say to McAndrew. And I'd also worked out where I was going to say it – somewhere Dwayne Thatcher wasn't.

We had English first thing next morning. Thatcher and McAndrew are in different classes, so I hung around in the corridor near McAndrew's room till I saw him coming. He saw me, too, and came towards me with a thoughtful expression on his face.

"Can I see you for a second?" I asked when he got near. He looked at me, dropped his bag on the floor, came over and stood in front of me. He's about five centimetres taller than me, I guess. He was tense, but he stood firm.

"Just wanted to say I'm sorry about last Friday," I told him. McAndrew didn't say anything, but moved his hands, which had been half-clenched by his sides, and put them in his pockets. "I shouldn't have used Tae Kwan Do like that," I went on. This was true. "I got carried away." This was Stacey's suggestion.

"You got carried away? Shit, I thought they'd

have to carry me away!" To my total amazement, McAndrew gave a sort of laugh. "Where did you learn to do that? Was it all Tae Kwan Do?"

"Yeah. But it's not the way you're supposed to use it." I felt I had to explain this, for some reason. "Tae Kwan Do's supposed to be about self-control, not fighting." McAndrew shrugged his shoulders ... okay, his broad shoulders. "So, like I say — I'm sorry I sprang it all on you. Our instructor would kick my bum if he knew."

"Yeah?" Kevin McAndrew gave a half-grin. I have to admit he's a good-looking guy, in a brutal sort of way. You can see why girls go for him. Some girls, anyway. "Might make up for the bruise on my bum. I'll see you coming next time, eh?"

We hadn't exactly shaken hands and looked each other firmly in the eye like good decent chaps. But I didn't feel any bad vibes coming from him. He picked up his bag and sloped off into his English class. I did the same.

Except that we didn't have English. Of course! It was the first of our Sex Education 'discussion' lessons. First time I've ever known a fifth form class to be all in the room and waiting *before* the bell went! Even Dwayne Thatcher was on time, slouching back in his seat, pretending he knew it all already.

It was actually a really useful lesson. Mrs Jennings took us, and she was more impressive than she sometimes is in PE. She's got a couple of teenagers of her own, so I guess that helps.

She started with the dramatic stuff — how the suicide rate among schoolgirl mothers is seven times as high as for other teenagers. Yeah, it made us sit up and listen.

She showed us a short video where one kid, who couldn't have been more than fifteen, was saying how she used to be so exhausted that she'd ram her baby's face into the bars of the cot to try and make it stop crying. Even Thatcher shut up after that.

Next time we're going to look at the 'Keeping Ourselves Safe' theme. And at some stage Mrs Jennings is going to get us to do a sort of experiment where you have to carry a raw egg round with you for a whole week, and keep it warm and safe. It's meant to show you what a full-time job it is, looking after a baby. I have this funny feeling that my egg could end up an omelette.

When I got to practice on Tuesday night, Trish was telling everyone that Frances had had her baby. "It's a dear little baby boy," Trish reported. You've probably noticed that babies are always dear and little; one of these days someone will have a cheap big baby, just to be different. Still, it's nice for Frances and Mr Frances, and it probably means another white belt for the club in eight or nine years.

There's another blue belt now. Leon's come back. Selwyn sensibly didn't say anything, and the others followed his example. But I wanted to clear up one thing that worried me.

"Did you come back because I flattened Kevin McAndrew?" I asked Leon before we lined up.

Leon looked at me and stuck his jaw out. "Nah. I came back because you tried to stop yourself from flattening him." He paused, then went on. "And because I want to flatten Dwayne Thatcher." I couldn't help laughing.

There were only four more club practices before tournament.

"Focus," Selwyn kept saying as he moved around. "Focus." I know what he means; when I'm training well, I sometimes feel as if light beams are pouring out of me and lining up on whatever event I'm working towards.

This Tuesday, Selwyn finished up with a long free-sparring session. He splits us into two lines. Then we spar with the person opposite for three minutes, before moving along one place and sparring with another, and so on.

It's excellent practice — you have to alter your tactics for the strength of Colin, the speed of Janelle, the cunning of Trish, the head-down, bull-at-a-gate technique of Leon, and Wiri the windmill. Even sparring with little Brenda is useful. (We've stopped calling her Atom Ant; now she's Mighty Mouse.) You learn to control everything you do to the last centimetre so you don't send the little nine-year-old flying the length of the hall.

"Hey, do you want to do some training after school tomorrow?" Stacey asked afterwards as we walked home holding hands. Mrs James and Ham were having coffee and bones at our place with Mum and Les, so Stacey was meeting them there. "You can come around to our place if you like."

Did I like? I liked. "Okay with your mum?" I checked.

"Course it is," Stacey said. "I told her I feel safe with you."

"Yeah — but am I safe with you?" I joked, and got the punch I expected.

The next day, after five depressing lessons and a not-too-unfriendly look from McAndrew, I rushed home, rushed though the shower, and rushed around to Stacey's. The bits of old car had vanished off the roadway outside the flats, but there were still enough oil stains to make Les feel right at home.

Ham consumer-tested the front door's strength from the inside when I rang. After he found I wasn't carrying any spare bits of brontosaurus, he went and lay on the rug, trying to look starved.

Stacey was wearing her gi — yellow belt and all. It made me feel a scruff in my old trackpants and T-shirt.

"I want to be used to wearing this when I fight in the tournament," she explained. "You've been wearing a gi so long, you never even think about it, but mine still feels strange when I put it on."

"You certainly look like you're into some serious training," I told her.

"I'm serious, all right," she said. She stepped towards me, closed her eyes and kissed me. Ham gave a bored yawn and settled down further on the rug.

"Chris?" murmured Stacey after a minute.

"Mmmmm?"

"Look out!" she warned me — too late. With her arms around my waist, Stacey shoulder-butted me in the ribs. I lurched half a step backwards, folded at the knees as I hit the sofa, and went sprawling across it on my back. Stacey sat down on the edge of the sofa and grinned in triumph.

"Am I allowed to do that at the tournament?" she asked.

"Only if you're fighting me," I managed to say. I reached my hands up, took her carefully by the ears, and pulled her down towards me. She went "ouch-ouch-ouch" all the way.

We stayed like that for a while; me with Stacey lying on my chest. If Mrs James walks in now, I thought, I'll have to pretend this is a new Tae Kwan Do move. I remembered the time a few years back when a mate and I were lying on our living room floor, sniggering our way through a girlie magazine he'd found at home. When Mum suddenly appeared, the only thing I could think of to do was to roll the magazine up as fast as I could, and start belting my mate with it, as if we were having a play fight. I half flattened the poor guy before he realised what I was doing. Then he chased me into my room — and I hid the magazine.

Stacey was better than any magazine. Her hair

kept falling across both our faces, and she kept blowing it away. My neck was getting an enormous crick in it, but I couldn't give a stuff. The Tae Kwan Do gi is only made of thin cotton, and with Stacey pressed close against me, I was storing up a lot of things to think about in my old age.

Stacey had gone quiet. Then she said again, "Chris?"

"I'm still here," I said, making out I was insulted. "Hadn't you noticed?"

She didn't laugh. In a voice that sounded a bit unnatural, she said against my chest, "You can touch me if you like."

My stomach went tight as a stone. I couldn't think of a thing to say. My left hand was around her shoulders. I started to move it very slowly down her back, over the surface of the gi. I could feel the little bumps of her spine, and her bra strap. Then the hollow at the base of her back, the elastic of her pants, and the curve of her bottom.

Stacey was trying to relax and lie still against me. I could feel her taking slow breaths. Then the moment my hand touched her bottom, she began to shake. And suddenly I knew exactly what I wanted to say.

"Look, Stacey — you don't have to."

"It's all right."

"No, wait! Look! Listen!" Make up your mind, Atkinson, the voice in my head complained. I raised myself up on the sofa and grabbed Stacey's hands.

Her face was turned away from me, but I could see she was chewing her bottom lip again. I put my hands on her shoulders, and turned her to face me.

"Look, I like kissing you, right? Right?" I gave her a shake. Stacey nodded, but still wouldn't look at me. "And of course I'd like to find out whether there really is a scar on your bum." Stacey made a noise that was part snort and part giggle. I drew a breath and went on. "And yeah, if you really want to know, of course I'd love to get you into bed." I distinctly saw the word "bed" fly across the room, ricochet off the wall, and land on the floor near Ham, who lifted his head and stared at us in a puzzled way. Then the word vanished out the window, where all the guys from the end flat could hear it.

Stacey was looking at me now, her pupils huge and black. She didn't say anything.

"Look, you're a really neat girl and everyone likes you and of course you turn me on and I like that! Right?" For God's sake, stop saying 'right', the voice in my head advised. And stop giving her a shake every time you say it.

Stacey, meanwhile, gave another little nod.

"But you don't do anything you don't want to do," I galloped on. "Right?" Damn — I did it again.

"I—" Stacey started to say. I held up my hand and she stopped. Such power! I thought.

"Look," I said for the umpteenth time, "you're special. Remember that. I intend to be around till I'm really old. Thirty-five, even."

185

Stacey was pressed up against me. She was shaking again, but it wasn't the frightened shaking of a few minutes back. It was a good shaking, if you can imagine what I mean.

"Chris," she said, in a wavery sort of voice, in between sniffs and hiccups. "Oh shit, Chris!"

I sat there with my arms around her for a few more minutes. My right leg had gone numb where it was bent underneath me. Stacey had stopped shaking. I waited to see if she'd tell me anything, but she didn't. Finally I spoke again, still all masterful.

"Now, I want you to do two things, and I want them done straight away. Ri— okay?"

Stacey nodded, and her hair tickled my nose.

"First, I want you to blow your nose, because I'm not having any woman dribbling and howling all down my training T-shirt."

Pause for some rustling and honking noises from down against my front. "And the second thing?" Stacey asked eventually.

I'd been waiting for this. I carefully took my arms away from her and collapsed slowly backwards across the sofa, like I'd been before.

"I'm exhausted after all this talking," I announced. "I feel quite faint. I think I may need mouth-to-mouth."

It's the first time I've ever been kissed by a girl who's been bawling. Mmmmm — salty.

186

Chapter 22

Training! Training! Ten days to tournament! Dig it in!

Stacey and I never did get any practice done on Wednesday afternoon. After a few minutes (which I haven't the slightest intention of telling you about), we just sat and held hands and talked. We didn't talk about anything special, except that everything we talked about seemed special. Then we kept holding hands while we walked a few blocks back towards my place, and Ham carried out a lamp post survey.

I couldn't stop smiling when I got home. I smiled while I did some weights, and I smiled while I did some dishes. "You're on good terms with the universe today," Mum remarked, looking rather pleased herself.

"Isn't he just?" agreed Lazyboy Les, doing a bit of his own smiling at Mum. Hell, we must have looked like a 'Have a happy day' sticker factory. "How are the Geography and History assignments coming along, Chris?"

Thanks, Les. Have you ever noticed how parents — and step-parents — have this genius for bringing you back to earth with a thump?

English on Thursday was a video about a play by Shakespeare called *King Lear*. I'd always thought 'leer' was the expression on Dwayne Thatcher's face, but you learn something every day.

These days I'm learning again how tight and exciting life can be. It always happens before a tournament; things get a brightly-lit feeling to them — what Selwyn calls "focus", I guess. Everything seems sharper, and seems to have more meaning.

Good practice on Thursday night. Selwyn took three of us one after the other — Janelle, then Leon, then me — and made us go through our patterns in front of the whole club. Then everyone had a chance to say what they thought we were doing badly or doing well.

Leon really concentrated, and people found a lot of good comments to make about him. Crafty, Selwyn!

Colin said he thought my ready stance looked as if I was ready to wrestle with my girlfriend. Stacey and I took care not to look at each other.

I'm working up to an edge. That's the way I imagine it. Something thin and sharp and bright; something that makes other people a bit wary. We finished the evening with some free-sparring, and Josh and I really went for each other. His eyes were narrow and his lips were pulled back around his mouthguard. He'd have scared the hell out of me if I hadn't been concentrating so hard. After Selwyn called "Stop", we kept standing with fists up for a second, before relaxing and bowing, and grinning at each other.

When I went back to sit in the circle around the sparring area, Stacey whispered, "Do I look as fierce as you and Josh when I'm sparring?"

I was flattered to learn that I looked fierce. I usually feel I don't have enough killer spirit. "No, you don't," I whispered back. "You look like you're ready to wrestle with your boyfriend."

Stacey was about to say something rude when Selwyn looked over at us and raised one eyebrow in a "Shut up" signal. We shut up.

"Good practice?" I said to Leon as we were leaving.

He looked embarrassed. "Not bad," he mumbled.

Stacey gave Leon a smile that made me feel envious. "Nice to have you back, Leon," she said. "I was getting bored with these other guys." Leon ducked his head, and Stacey winked at me.

"Watch yourself, ya little turd," I told Leon, acting jealous. Partly acting, anyway. "Just keep your distance from this girl, or I might have to lean on you."

"You and whose air force?" Leon asked, and

jumped on his bike with a smile from earlobe to earlobe. Stacey gave me a poke in the ribs with her finger, took my hand and marched me off.

Mrs James was doing some overtime cleaning, and had arranged to pick up Stacey from our place a bit later. Les had been going to drive them home, but a back leg fell off his car today, and there weren't any spare parts in the antique shops. So we went straight home to Les and Mum.

Fairly straight home, anyway. Halfway along the right-of-way where we'd held hands the first time, Stacey stopped and said, "We'd better not embarrass the olds later on, eh? So you'd better kiss me goodnight now . . ." Well, you know me — I always do what a lady tells me. And anyway, it's kinda neat to have a girl actually tell you to kiss her!

Mum and Les treat Stacey like one of our family now. And after some of Les's particularly sick jokes this night, Stacey and Mum ganged up on him. They said he was a sexist pig and a male chauvinist. Finally, Les got down on hands and knees, crawled under the table, and announced he wasn't coming out till the world was safe for defenceless men.

Les was still under the table when Mrs James and Ham arrived. Mrs James looked surprised. Ham looked interested, and joined Les to see if he had a secret food supply hidden there. There wasn't enough room for them both so Les came out again. Mrs James smiled at him and Mum and me, but saved her biggest smile for Stacey.

"We've got another Sex Education lesson today," I told Mum and Les next morning.

Les put on a shocked expression. "I never even thought of sex when I was at school," he said.

"You never even thought of education when you were at school," Mum grinned.

"You just wait!" Les smirked. "You could be in for a surprise." He wouldn't tell us any more, but went out to the garage, singing 'Roll Out the Barrel', while Mum and I yelled that we'd roll out the barrel if he were in it.

The Sex Ed lesson was in our English period, like last time. And, like last time, the whole class was on time again. Stacey came in just after I did, and while we talked, a few kids around us went nudge-nudge wink-wink.

"Sexual safety," Mrs Jennings announced at the start of the lesson. What she said and what we talked about during the next thirty or so minutes certainly made some of us sit up and listen. Again, I was impressed by Mrs Jennings. She knows her stuff, and she cares about it. She made sure she got heard, and she made sure other people had the chance to get heard.

We talked about the contraceptive side of sexual safety, and Mrs Jennings was pretty strong on how she reckoned the safest contraceptive of all is still the word "No".

"I'll write it on the board for those of you who

191

have spelling problems," she said. She wrote it in red chalk, in letters about a metre high. Even Dwayne Thatcher should have been able to follow that.

We talked about personal safety, and the pressures on teenagers to have sex even if they're scared or don't want to. Some of the kids talked about a programme they had seen on TV about date rape — the idea some guys have that if a girl says she'll go out with them, or if they pay for things while they're out, it gives them the right to expect sex in return.

Then we got onto the sexual molestation side. Mrs Jennings was telling us how most girls and women — and boys — who get attacked aren't ambushed in a dark alley by some stranger. They're usually molested by someone they already know. Often it's a relative, or a family friend, or someone like that.

"It's the sudden loss of trust that makes it so dreadful for the victim," Mrs Jennings said. "Someone they may have liked and trusted has suddenly done this awful thing to them. They don't believe they can really feel safe with anybody, ever again." Warning bells started echoing in my mind.

Someone wanted to know the sorts of effects that sexual molestation might have on the victim later in life.

"There are as many effects as there are people involved," Mrs Jennings said. "Some people are able to get over the worst of it very quickly, thanks to counselling or lots of support from their families. Others stay frightened and shocked for years. They feel betrayed. They can't bear to come near anyone or be touched, because even the most innocent touch can bring everything back." More echoes.

Mrs Jennings looked towards me for a second. She hesitated, then said, "Maybe if I read you one piece from this book I have here."

The part she read us was written by a girl who'd been sexually molested by her father when she was eleven. She'd tried to tell her mother, but her mother wouldn't believe her, and said she was just making up stories. The girl kept running away from home to try and escape her father, who was still molesting her. When she was older, she met a guy and got keen on him, but she wouldn't let him even kiss her. The moment he tried, she went into fits of screaming and crying. When he finally gave up and stopped seeing her, she tried to kill herself. Luckily a welfare agency got to her in time, and she was able to start putting her life back together.

It was a bloody disturbing story. I sat there just staring at my desk, and I think most of the others were the same. There were a few gasps and shuffles at the worst parts. Even Thatcher forgot to yawn.

Mrs Jennings finished reading. She looked towards me again. Does she know what I'm thinking? I wondered.

One of the guys on the other side of the room started on about how he reckoned all sexual molesters of children should be castrated. Someone else reckoned that was as bad as what the molesters had done; if you were going to worry about their victims as people, you had to worry about the offenders too.

Mrs Jennings seemed to be only half paying attention to this new discussion. She looked in my direction a third time. And finally I realised she wasn't looking at me. She was looking beyond me, at Stacey. Stacey, who had sat down behind me at the start of the lesson, saying, "Now behave yourself, Chris Atkinson, or I'll kick you in the bum."

I had enough sense not to turn around and gawp. But as the discussion over castration-with-a-rusty-pocketknife got louder on the other side of the room, I deliberately elbow-nudged my ballpoint off the desk onto the floor. I bent down to pick it up and, as I straightened up again, I snatched a quick look at Stacey.

She was crying. Her hands were over her face and she wasn't moving or making a sound, but she was crying so much that the tears were running down the curve of her cheeks and onto the inside of her wrists. I saw it all in one glance, even the fingernails cut short for Tae Kwan Do and the soft blue vein at the side of her neck.

Nobody else except Mrs Jennings and me seemed to have noticed her, but it was only a matter of time before the others did. I waited a few seconds till Mrs Jennings looked towards Stacey again, then I half rose in my seat to catch her eye, and jerked my head towards Stacey.

I'll never underestimate Mrs Jennings again. She gave me a quick nod, then immediately changed the discussion and drew everybody's attention back to the other side of the room.

I stood up, turned to Stacey and took her elbow. I whispered, "Come on, Shorty." She didn't say a thing, just got to her feet and came with me.

Luckily we were near the back of the classroom. Hardly any kids saw us, and I don't think those who did, realised what was happening.

Once we reached the corridor, I let go of her elbow and put my arm around her shoulders. We went along the corridor, out through the double doors, and round to a sheltered end wall of the classroom block. We sat down on one of the seats. Stacey pushed her face into the hollow of my neck and, as I put my other arm around her as well, she cried as if she were going to cry forever.

She didn't go quite forever, which was just as well, but my regulation glamour-grey school shirt collar was pretty well soaked by the time she did finish. It must have been about five minutes before her crying slowed down into sobs and sniffs and hiccups.

And into words. "That girl — I was twelve — Mum's boyfriend — kicked him out when I told — still scared — even after . . ." She stopped talking and fumbled round in the sleeve of her school jumper for a hanky. She found it and blew hell out of it for a few seconds. Then she put her head back against my shoulder and gave a huge, long, shuddering sigh.

"It's all right," I told her. "I already knew."

Stacey looked up at me. Her face was pink and puffy, except in the places where it was white and wet. I'd have kissed her right then and there if I hadn't thought there was probably a school rule against kissing girls during lesson time. "How did you know?" she asked. "I thought only Mum knew. Her and Mrs Jennings."

"Well, I didn't think it was just my B.O. that upset you so much when I touched you those times," I said. "And you did sort of tell me once." As I spoke, I remembered how I'd seen her coming out of Mrs Jennings' office during those weeks after she arrived at school, and thought she was just a snobby new kid who hated being in a strange place. Wrong again, Chris Atkinson.

Stacey put her head on my shoulder again and was silent for a few more minutes. Then: "I'm glad someone else knows. I'm glad you know."

She didn't say anything more for a while, just leaned there while her breathing slowly calmed down. After a while she put one of her hands against my side.

"I do like your ribs," she murmured.

I heard the bell go for the start of interval, and heard kids moving in the corridors. A few minutes later, there were voices around the corner from us. Mrs Jennings appeared with a couple of girls from our class.

"Poor Stacey!" Mrs Jennings exclaimed. "Aren't

migraines awful things? Did you take your pills? Feeling better now?"

I stared at Mrs Jennings in surprise. I didn't know Stacey suffered from migraines. Then I caught the look Mrs Jennings gave me.

"Uh, yeah," I gabbled. "Yeah, I think she is a bit better." See, I can lie as well as any teacher. "She's still feeling pretty groggy, though."

"Of course," Mrs Jennings nodded wisely. "Well, Michelle and Sue can take you to the sick bay, Stacey dear. You have a bit of a lie down."

The other two girls helped Stacey stand up, and the three of them headed off. Mrs Jennings watched them go for a second. I heard her mutter, "I shouldn't have tried it." Then she turned round to me, said, "You're an all right kid, Chris Atkinson," and followed them.

I sat there for a moment, feeling embarrassed but pleased. Then I stood up, straightened my wet collar, soggy jersey and crumpled shirt-front, and started wandering back towards the classroom and my bag.

As I came round the corner of the end wall, I met Dwayne Thatcher. He was standing watching Stacey and Mrs Jennings and the other girls as they went in through the double doors.

"Geez, Atkinson, you're a real stud, aren't ya?" he sneered. "Getting the girls out of class for a quick grope now, eh?"

I didn't even have to think. My left leg and my right arm came forward together, and I hit him with a

197

straight lunge punch, right on the nerve centre under his ribcage. He went down on the grass and lay there on his side, squawking and pulling his knees up as he dragged in air.

Two other figures had come round the corner in time for our little scene. They had growing grins on their faces.

"Hell, I'll have to learn that one!" said Kevin McAndrew.

"You beat me to it!" said Leon. But he didn't look too sad about it.

Chapter 23

It was quite a week. Thanks to Mrs Jennings, nobody else at school seemed to have noticed Stacey crying in Sex Ed. A few kids have noticed the way she and I have been sitting together most lunchtimes, and holding hands if we leave school together in the afternoon, but the comments are nearly all friendly. There's a few bitchy ones, but they're not worth worrying about.

Stacey's not kidding herself that her fears are over. She'll still need lots of talking and comfort.

I guess I can never really understand what it's been like for her. I know Mrs Jennings has been round to see her and Mrs James a couple of times since, and Stacey says they're all going to see a sexual abuse counsellor soon. She just wishes she'd gone before, when her Mum wanted her to.

Meanwhile, she looks and talks as if she's starting to step out into the sunlight, and something black and horrible is fading away behind her.

I told Mum and Les about her mother's boyfriend. I'd asked Stacey if I could when she and I went for a walk together last weekend. Stacey had stopped so suddenly that Ham, who was trotting along behind looking for dead dinosaurs, banged into us. It made us stagger and it made Ham rumble. Stacey said, "Would you, Chris? I'd like your Mum to know. Or would it be better if my Mum . . ?"

But I wanted to do it. I found Mum and Les watching TV when I got home. (I rattled the front doorknob first, so they had time to look middle-aged and respectable.) They sat and didn't say a thing while I told them about what had happened at school, and what Stacey had told me when she was crying.

Then Mum said, "Poor Stacey. Poor Karen," and hugged me as if I was the one who'd been hurt.

Later in the week, when Stacey came around to our place on her way to Tae Kwan Do, Mum just put her arms around her and held her really tight. Les and I looked firmly into the distance to prove we didn't have a pricking in our manly eyes, then Stacey suddenly came over and gave Les a hug as well. And Les couldn't think of a single joke!

Mum helped him out. "Like stepfather, like stepson," she said, and smiled at him and me.

I didn't apologise to Dwayne Thatcher for decking him. In fact, I keep thinking back to the absolutely perfect way that lunge punch landed. He gives me poison looks if we come anywhere near each other at school, and I still swivel my head round in a full circle if I think he's anywhere behind me. But otherwise I couldn't care less.

He and Kevin McAndrew still hang round together. McAndrew's not too bad, I realise now; he's a guy who'd be quite an asset at Tae Kwan Do. But friendships are funny things: you can never tell which way they'll go.

I keep thinking about Stacey, too, and the things that have happened between us in the last three months. (Only three months?) She's helped me. I hope I've helped her. I hope someone, someday, somehow, can help Dwayne Thatcher!

All through this last week, I've trained and concentrated and psyched myself up, till I'm almost jumping out of my skin with fitness and readiness to go. Selwyn's pleased with me, I can tell. On our final training night before tournament, he said just one word to me: "Control." I know what he meant; there's no way I'm going to make a nerd of myself like I did last time.

Actually, I was grateful that Selwyn didn't say more. I was scared he'd somehow heard about my little efforts with McAndrew and Thatcher. He likes Tae Kwan Do to be used only for the right reasons. I asked Leon not to say anything, and he grinned when he said, "Course I won't! I'm not stupid, you know." Maybe he's not.

When I got home from training Mum was making her shopping list.

"Do you want to cook that pork casserole again on Thursday?" Mum asked Les. Then added, "It's a bit expensive, though."

Les looked smug. "I won't be able to cook on Thursday. But we can still have it, if you like — it doesn't matter if it's expensive."

Mum and I both stared at him. "Oh, didn't I tell you? I'm starting work at the Polytech the day after tomorrow. They want me to be their general handyman and vehicle mechanic."

I left the dining room about five minutes later, when the scene was getting too sloppy for words. Mum was patting Les's hand and cooing things like "Marvellous . . . clever . . . always knew you could."

Les was trying to look modest, and saying, "Ah well, can't be on holiday all your life, I s'pose."

I had to laugh, though. When you think of the state of Les's car, it's hard to imagine him making a living fixing other people's things!

Chapter 24

We travelled up to the tournament last night in cars this time, instead of a minibus.

We met at the hall after school on Friday. I think our whole Tae Kwan Do club was there, except for Colin, who was working. He says that if any of us win a medal, we can have an hour's free drive in his big rig. If it's me (touch wood!) I might use it to cart Les's car away for a quiet funeral service somewhere.

Even the ones who aren't competing in this tournament came along to see us off. Mighty Mouse Brenda was there, dancing around everyone and pretending to punch Josh on the backside — till Josh threatened to tread on her!

Frances had brought her new baby along, and Trish, Stacey, Janelle and the other females all cooed over it. I kept well away. I've got nothing against babies — Mum claims I was one myself, once — but I reckon they should be kept behind barbed wire till they're fully house-trained.

Stacey and I sat in the back of Trish's car and held hands all the way up, except for the time Stacey slipped her arm around the small of my back, up under my T-shirt, and tickled me on the ribs. I went "Aarghh!", and then had to tell Trish and Mrs James in the front seat that I'd got a cramp in my foot. Wiri, who was on the other side of me, gave a knowing grin and was opening his mouth to say something till I elbowed him in the ribs.

Yeah, Mrs James has come up with us. I should have realised she wouldn't miss out on the chance to feel proud of her daughter. The guys with tats from the end flat are looking after Ham till we get back tonight. They jumped at the chance: said it would boost their image no end to be seen with the fiercest rottweiler in town. Ham kept looking around as if he was wondering who they were talking about.

There's a really good feeling among our club members up here at the tournament. Last night we all slept in sleeping bags on the floor of Selwyn's sister's living room. Guys at one end; girls at the other.

Trish announced "I'll be patrolling the middle with a searchlight and a machine gun. So will Karen," — Trish nodded at a smiling Mrs James — "so keep your distance."

We all booed and hissed and then did what we were told. It was weird knowing that Stacey was sleeping so close by; I just hope it wasn't her who snored!

I met Rick again this morning — the guy who beat me last tournament. "Hi," he said. "What grade are you in?"

"Still welterweight," I told him. "I'm still skinny."

Rick breathed a sigh of relief. "I'm light-middleweight now," he said. "Geez, I'm glad I don't have to fight you again. Dunno how I won last time." He gave Stacey an interested look and went off to the side of the hall where his club was sitting. I knew exactly how he won last time — he fought better than I did! But I didn't mind hearing him put it that way — especially in front of Stacey.

So far this morning, there've been three preliminary bouts with our club members in them. Janelle won hers: she's medal material, all right. Leon fought really well against an older and more experienced kid, and when he got beaten he stepped straight forward and shook the other guy's hand. We clapped him all the way back to his seat.

Then Stacey had her first bout. She just flowed through it, the way she did through her grading. Her opponent was a yellow belt green tab, against Stacey's yellow belt, but I never doubted for a second she was going to win. Some day she's going to be so much better than me, and it doesn't worry me a bit.

I sat there watching her stand and lean and stretch, and all the time I was thinking how good she makes me feel.

I've no way of knowing what'll happen with me and Stacey. I'm not worried about that, either. Besides, I can always let Mum do the worrying! What are mothers for?

We could be a long-term thing: that'd be just great as far as I'm concerned. But anything could change — Mrs James' career; Stacey's career; even my career, if some employer is willing to take the risk! Stacey and I are still young. We've still got things to learn. (My Geography and English teachers both told me last week that I've got lots of things to learn.)

I've been thinking a few world-shattering thoughts like this while we cheer Stacey's win, and while I do my leg-stretching and warm-up exercises. I'm next. I've seen the guy I'm fighting in my preliminary bout: he looks bigger and stronger than me (again!). In fact he looks a bit like Kevin McAndrew. He's going to be hard to beat.

Selwyn's been helping me warm up, holding his hands up, palms outwards, while I smack punches against them as fast as I can. "Strong legs, Chris," he says quietly, while I tie my body-padding and helmet on. I know what he means: if you force your legs to keep driving and pumping, you can last through anything.

The gong goes for the start of my bout. My opponent and I walk over to the competition area marked on the hall floor with bright red insulating tape. We try not to look at each other.

The crowd goes silent, the way they're supposed to

do, while we bow to the four judges and to the referee.

We turn and bow to each other. We both go into a fighting stance; knees slightly bent, weight evenly spread, fists up, elbows guarding ribs. His forearms are wider apart than they should be; there's a gap for a spinning reverse kick there. I take a vast breath from the bottom of my stomach, in through my nose, charging myself up with oxygen.

The gong sounds again, and the hall is a burst of cheers and shouts and yells of encouragement. I hear Stacey's clear voice calling out for me, and a great rush of excitement and warmth sweeps up inside me as I start forward.

Things are going to be fine.